CREDOMANICS

An Act of Faith

Bijumon Jacob

PARTRIDGE
A Penguin Company

Partridge books may be ordered through booksellers or by contacting:

Partridge India
Penguin Books India Pvt.Ltd
11, Community Centre, Panchsheel Park, New Delhi 110017
India
www.partridgepublishing.com
Phone: 000.800.10062.62

CREDOMANICS

CONTENTS

Dedicated

To those who live their belief

1

The Farm

The early morning rays were peeping through the leaves of the nutmeg trees around the lone farmhouse on the hill. Clad in khaki shorts and black loose fitting T-shirt, James let the flock of country chicken out of the poultry almost a hundred feet behind the house. Amidst the clucking of the happy lot that spread around the farm, he heard Avira shout from the kitchen.

"There is a call for you!"

This was very surprising as hardly anyone had called him in the past five years and never at such an early hour. James washed his hands at the water pipe cocked outside the house. He went into the living room where the phone was. Avira, who was cooking tapioca and fish curry in the kitchen, came out with a wooden ladle in his hand. He had a red colour bathing towel rolled and tied around his waist holding his flower printed *kitex lungi* safely in its place and he used the same to dry his wet palms. His bare upper body showed off well defined muscles that didn't match his current job as a cook.

"He said he'd call back in a couple of minutes."

"Who was it?"

"He didn't say. I thought there was a sense of urgency in his voice. Sort of tense."

"I don't deal with emergencies, Avira. Not anymore." James sat next to the phone and lit a Goldflake Kings. "Where are the others?"

"Leo is not back from the Dairy and Joe is still snoring loud enough to match the grinder in the kitchen."

Leo was the early bird among the four men. He got up early every morning to milk the five cows and drive down to the local town's corporative dairy.

Joe was still sluggish from last night's party and would only wake up in time for breakfast.

"Asshole drank too much last night," said Avira.

It was when they celebrated the anniversary of setting up the twenty acre farm and everyone was entitled to loosen up. A couple of country chickens were roasted; homemade gooseberry arrack and spicy pork gravy were the highlight of the celebration. It was also a night when flashes of their lives had popped up again and again propelled by the strong arrack, only to be forgotten and not talked about in the morning.

The phone rang again.

"Hello, this is James. Who is this?"

"His Excellency Reverend Matthias, Archbishop of Kunnamkulam, wants to talk to you, urgently." said an unsteady hurried voice, "I am Fr. Vincent George, his secretary."

"Holy shit!" James murmured. "You know, I don't even go to Church anymore nor do I interact with the so called Excellencies. How did you get my number?"

"His Excellency Rev . . ."

"Cut the crap Father. What do you want?"

There rose a pause, some low whispers followed by a more powerful baritone replacing the sheepish priest.

"Jamie, this is Matthias Pulimoottil." The voice resounded with familiarity and solemnity. James could now work out the connections in his mind. A long-time friend, the youngest bishop in the Syrian Catholic Church was now an Archbishop.

"Your Excellency . . ." It had been almost ten years since they last spoke to each other. Much had changed from their seminary days.

"Now you cut the crap. It is Matthias. I need to meet you."

"I am sorry; I didn't recognize you at first. It'd be good to catch up. I would love to show you around our farm but it seems you are now a busy Archbishop."

"Another time mate and if I lose my job I can come and stay with you for as long as you want," the Archbishop suddenly got serious, "I have to meet you urgently."

"I am some hundred kilometres from the Archbishop's house of Kunnamkulam. When do you want to meet, and why?"

"Now. As quickly as the Merc that is waiting outside your farm can get you here."

"Shucks, what the hell is going on? Can we not talk about it over the phone?" James looked through the window at a sleek black Mercedes Benz parked outside. "I have a farm to run."

"No. Not over the phone. Put on some fresh clothes, switch on your bloody cell phone and join Kuruvila, the driver. I will see you in a couple of hours." Before his Excellency put the phone down, James could hear a cell phone ringing at the other end.

James sat back on the sofa and composed his thoughts. Avira, who was almost done with the cooking, sensed something serious was afoot and left the fish curry on low fire. He came and sat on the chair opposite James.

The four-wheel drive Mahindra 500 pulled up and parked near the portico. Leo walked briskly into the living room and paused at his friend's worried expressions.

"I think I need to start to Kunnamkulam right away. Let's all have a quick breakfast. Call the driver in, he must be hungry too." James went into his room.

Leo gave Avira a puzzled look before his friend filled him in about the news and explained why there was a Mercedes waiting outside.

Avira invited the driver for breakfast but he refused and settled for a cup of tea which he slurped standing at the portico.

Joe showed up stretching and blinking just as James came out of his room with a backpack, dressed in blue Jeans and a white T-shirt.

"I missed the alarm this morning. The cock didn't crow," Joe looked sleepily at Avira. "What time is it?"

"Time for breakfast, mister. Blame the seven or eight neat larges that you had last night and not the poor cock. And it is not gentlemanly to blame someone posthumously. You ate him yesterday for dinner!" Avira placed a bowl of steaming fish curry on the table.

"Ah! You killed my alarm clock, rascal!" Joe went away looking for his toothbrush and paste. He came back quickly when the other four started breakfast.

"Now, listen," James spoke authoritatively and got their full attention. "I've got an urgent meeting with the Archbishop Matthias of Kunnamkulam. I've known the guy for a long time but we've not been in touch since he was made bishop. He has sent a car to pick me up."

"Bishop with a Merc?" Leo smiled.

James ignored the question though it had already crossed his mind.

"I am leaving right away and I want you guys to switch on your cell phones and make sure they're fully charged."

Cell phones were usually switched off in the farm as these farmers did not wish to be accessible or available to anyone else.

James turned to Joe, "I need you to go online and dig up what Archbishop Matthias has been doing for the last few years, officially and unofficially, everything you can lay your hands on."

Joe nodded.

James finished off his hot coffee in one gulp, picked up the backpack and went outside.

The next minute the Mercedes sped off leaving the other three men still figuring out the sudden change in their otherwise serene life.

2

The Archbishop of Kunnamkulam

Sitting in the comfort of the air-conditioned Benz, James was annoyed that his daily routine and peace had been disturbed. Over the last five years he and his three friends have been immersed in what they liked best: farming. The farm covered twenty acres on one side of the hill and had a stream passing through the western part. They raised an assortment of cows, one hundred odd poultry; forty rabbits and a Doberman called Nosey, and enjoyed their life away from the cities and towns they hated. And the people they hated.

Matthias had been integral to the first part of James' life. He reminded him of classrooms, headmaster, school festivals, church bells, morning prayers, cassocks, crosses, sacristy and the sweetness of Mass wine.

James had abandoned the 'Call' or as he often said, never got the 'Call' at all. Matthias had been 'Called', anointed and 'hierarchised' by the administrative Church, and was now an Archbishop—the youngest in the rite at the age of forty. From a batch of thirty that entered the seminary, only five went on to become the shepherds of the Lord, most leaving in the first five years. James had lasted a good eight and then, when he could no more handle the cognitive dissonance—huge disparity between the core of faith and actual practice, had walked out—before being shown the door by the Rector.

As they reached the valley and entered the National Highway, James asked the driver to pull up by a roadside tea-shop. He ordered a strong tea, picked up a *'parippu vada'* from the stale panelled show case and munched.

"Tea?" he asked the driver who nodded.

"*Mashe*, make it two." he said loudly to the tea shop guy who was now skilfully pouring the tea from the copper cup to the glass, drawing and arch in the air. James lit a Kings and took two deep drags. January is pleasant, neither hot nor too cool around this area unlike the northern part of the country. Or unlike Chennai where it was hot, hotter and hottest throughout the year.

On a bench outside the tea shop sat a middle aged man in *lungi* and sleeveless faded vest reading the day's *Manorama* Newspaper. James looked over his shoulder and saw the main headings.

"Vatican to verify Miracles of Blessed Chalakkudi Josappachan."

The clergy always managed to get to the front page of dailies *Manorama* and *Deepika*.

The two column write up was on Father Joseph who lived in the pre-independence time and had done some good work among the sick and old destitute in and around Chalakkudi. A few years ago he was declared Blessed by the Holy Catholic Church and was a favourite for Sainthood. Vatican has not been very generous with granting such pompous titles to brown skinned Brethren and it took much lobbying and grinding evaluations. The Pope sends high ranking officials to verify the so-called miracles the faithful have experienced by invoking the dead priest. Officials of the Holy See were almost certain that such claims were often fabricated both by compulsion from the local clergy and the so called benefactor's urging to hog some limelight.

James paid the shopkeeper and motioned the driver that they start right away. He stamped the half-finished cigarette butt and hurried off to the car. When they reached the Archbishop's *Aramana*, James was immediately received by Fr. Vincent George.

"Mr James Mathew?"

James smiled.

"You are eagerly expected. This way, please," Father Vincent waved his hand. He was a timid, clean-shaven priest in his mid-thirties and wore a white cassock and equally white row of teeth exposed in a humble smile, trying unsuccessfully to hide his nervousness.

James was led straight to the office of Archbishop Matthias, who stood up and walked around the huge teak panelled table to welcome James. He noticed that the luxuries of Catholic Church had not succeeded in expanding the waistline of this man. In his white cassock and broad purple girdle, Matthias was tall and handsome, fit as a fiddle.

"My man!" Matthias cried as he embraced his friend.

"You still look exactly the same!" said his friend. The Archbishop signalled his secretary to leave them alone, and then picked up two cups and saucers from the side table and a hot flask. He poured steaming coffee into the cups and gestured James to take a chair while he sat gracefully on his swirling high back leather seat.

He threw three newspapers on the table—*Deepika*, *The Hindu* and *Malayala Manorama*—for James to see and placed his index finger on the Josepachan news item.

"Heard of this?"

"Not really, just had a glance along the way."

"The dignitaries from the Vatican were supposed to be staying here last night and visit various locations to interview some folks later today. They reached the Karippur Airport via Mumbai yesterday. The flight was delayed for an hour, nothing unusual in this part of the country. The two officials were picked up at the airport but never reached their destination."

"What happened?"

"The BMW X6 along with the two dignitaries, and a priest were last seen at Kondotty town. Around midnight I got a call from the Malappuram Police saying that the BMW was found abandoned in a coconut grove near Kizhisseri about 8 kilometres from airport. There is absolutely no trace of the occupants." Matthias took a deep breath.

"Being the Pope's representatives from the Vatican, are they entitled to diplomatic status?"

"Yes. They are Vatican's Diplomats and the government's official guests."

"So the Police are on active look out, they may have a scent already. C.I. Kunju Koya is the smart officer among the lot." James opined still wondering why Matthias has sent so urgently for him.

The Archbishop continued as though he did not hear James at all. "After two more hours I got another call. It was them, the Naxals! They want to trade the two high ranking diplomats for five of the worst criminals in captivity."

"So, they have spelled out their demands in the first call? That's strange and amateurish."

"They are desperate. These five were their best fighters; they were behind many of the deadly attacks in various parts of the country. That is, until a brave IPS officer chased them to the corners of Tamilnadu and captured them alive in the Sathyamangalam forests," a knowing smile flashed briefly on Matthias countenance.

"That officer is no longer in service. He has vowed never to return to the rotten Police Service!" James said emphatically looking away.

"But you are the one who knows how they think and act. Maybe even where they could go." His Excellency leaned forward.

"You do not know the whole story, only what was reported by the media. When I arrested them I was still a staunch sympathizer of their cause. I made a commitment to the people of that area, without who my team's efforts would have been futile."

"I thought you had a score to settle."

"On the contrary, my friend! I had a seven point plan to rehabilitate the ecosystem that supported and sustained the naxalites once I got the criminals behind bars. I had a commitment to the folks that were being ignored, trampled and kicked around. Frankly, the naxals have a nobler cause, much nobler to me than what your three priests have! You wouldn't be surprised if I myself wouldn't let those five guys out to take on the politicians of Kerala, Tamilnadu and Karnataka ! All of them had vowed to support me rehabilitate the affected villagers when I captured the naxals," grunted James.

"But instead you chose self-imposed exile! You ran away from the system." Matthias was now animated. "Let me be frank with you, man, you are the bravest coward I have ever seen! You should have confronted them, convinced them and changed the system than to go on a long leave when demands were not met."

"Do I care?"

"You do. You ran away from the girl you loved dearly as a fifteen year old, because she 'seemed' to like someone else. You wouldn't stay and fight it out with her so-called lover. And then what happened?"

"There was no such lover," James admitted.

"Yes. Elena loved you and only you. I had the misfortune of knowing the heartache of a girl who loved you madly. You are the loser!"

"Yes, I am." James gave him a diffident 'what-if' kind of look.

"You spent eight years in the seminary training for priesthood, oscillating between the Lord of the Church and your own consciousness. You saw them as opposites and instead of learning to reconcile, or fight to bring them together. And then you ran away!" Matthias got up from his chair, walked up slowly and sat on the table. He towered over James. "How long will you continue this flight?"

"Yes. I escaped from the Seminary. I ran away from the Police Force too! And I am not going to come back to this corrupted policing just because some fucking diplomats from your beloved Vatican have been caged up by the Naxalites. I don't care at all about them. And I don't care about the One who sent them here either. He might be your boss but he's not mine!"

James got up and went close to Matthias, looking him straight in the eyes, he smiled. "Frankly, I do not think these Vatican's officials add much value to this world. You can create a lot of noise with the Police about rescue efforts, but let those priests die in captivity. Then you can blame the Police for letting down the Catholic Church and tell everyone that the Communist government is antichristian and pro-naxalite! They never really cared for the safety of Christian missionaries. After all Marxists claim that they are atheists, right? Isn't that a good spin enough for you?"

"There is value in every human life. I am not asking you to fight the naxals and release the kidnapped priests. I want you to negotiate with them." The Archbishop said plainly.

"Why should I?"

"You will save the Indian government and the Church in India from huge embarrassment. Not to mention saving three innocent lives that have done nothing to hurt the cause of the Naxalites."

"I am not interested. A priest is dispensable. I lost 5 men in my last operation in Sathyamangalam, all valiant defendants of the law of this land!" James was agitated.

"Will it convince you if I said that . . ." Matthias rose from where he sat and placed both hands on the other man's shoulders, ". . . the priest who was kidnapped along with the officials is Zacharia Tharakan?"

"Zach Tharakan . . ." James was stunned and Matthias waited to let the information sink into the rough and tough ex-cop, who has also once been a revolutionary seminarian. James moved back slowly and sat back on the chair.

James took out the Kings packet, looked at Matthias who motioned dismissively to go ahead, lighted one and exhaled, adding smoke to the tension in the air of the Archbishop's office.

3

The Three Musketeers

"You are in big trouble, gentlemen." Matthias Lukose said gravely to the two anxious souls standing tensely in the mango grove behind St Margaret's High School. The weary tenth graders, James Mathew and Johny Joseph, had confessed to him all about their misadventure that morning. Matthias was the student representative of their class, the school secretary, the best student in school and, of course, their best friend.

"Are you guys crazy? Pulling out the pins from the girls' hair! Is this some attention seeking behaviour or plain desperation?" Matthias leaned forward and looked into their eyes. They looked down.

James thought it was the coolest thing to do in the morning. To stand in the staircase and pull out the pins that held the carefully tied hair together, watching the surprised and harassed looks of the junior girls when it came loose on their shoulders and face. He felt the parents of girls did a big disservice to the "men" in school by tying up the babes' hair. They looked so pretty with it loose.

To the boys' surprise, most girls enjoyed this morning drill, some taunting them with a mock reprimanding look. The guys were thrilled.

In the kick of such encouragement, they had the audacity to play the same prank with Maria, who was haughty, high nosed and amply endowed for an eighth grader. Her mother, Catherine Madam, was the math's teacher and a nightmare to all the students that she ever taught. She had sharp and narrow eyes that pierced everyone in her class and a wide waistline, which swung wobbly as she walked in agitation.

Johny was already tugging on Maria's pretty pink hairpin when James realized who the target was and pulled his friend back instinctively. In the ensuing confusion, Johny had tripped, pulling the raging girl down with him. He landed on his bum with her on his lap, skirt up. In an instant reaction, James had pulled Johny from under the dame, dashed off and stopped only after they had reached their classroom.

"Did she see you?" Asked Matthias gravely, looking to give them an alibi.

"I don't think so; we were on the stairs and moved from behind her."

"She landed on my lap. She would have found out who I was." Johny swallowed hard.

"As if she is familiar to sitting on your lap. You were zipped up, right?"

The duo had had no problems with Joseph Chandi, the now retired headmaster, who would settle everything with three whacks below the knee. The new headmaster, however, terrorized the troublesome students that were sent to his office with his misplaced sense of humour and generous use of vulgar vocabulary. Cherian Kora enjoyed spanking with his tongue and prided himself about being a writer of 'repute', having written two '*painkili*' serialised novels in some shady weekly.

Maybe Cherian would even call the boys' parents to school to complain directly to the adults. They could not afford to do that, not for teasing girls!

They needed complete support from their class secretary who, with his impeccable behaviour, was a favourite of all the teachers and, most importantly, the Principal, Cherian the novelist.

As the boys dreaded, the peon was sent to the last class to get the two trouble makers. When they approached the door marked 'Head Master', they saw Catherine Madam walking out, swaying more violently than usual with anger written all over her ugly face.

"May we come in, sir?" said the two in unison.

"Come in Romeos!" Grunted Cherian mockingly from behind the desk that hid most of his prosperous mid region but left his puffy cheeks and slumping shoulders exposed. He wore a *khadi* white shirt like the one politicians wear.

To Cherian's left, standing in silent submission, was their friend Matthias. His expression did not give them any consolation. They looked at Cherian with a pleading smile trying to invoke some sleeping sympathy in the monster.

"What do you guys think of yourselves? You think this school is some fish market?" The scolding was bearable so far.

He then stood up and the boys kept looking down but they could sense Cherian gradually transforming into his novelist self.

"Suppose one of these girls has a muscular enough father or brother or uncle, what do you think they will do? They would chop off your little pricks and shove them up your sniffing noses! Or maybe up your backside! Didn't you peep at their cleavage while you conducted this shameless act of yours?" He tried to bend down to look them in the eyes but his bulging tummy only allowed so much, still his face was close to theirs now. James could feel the foul smell of Charminar Cigarette emanating from the older man's mouth along with the fouler words he shot at them. Johny was now wondering how he could have missed the opportunity that Cherian had suggested and cursed himself for being stupid.

"We . . . were just playing sir. Didn't mean to hurt or tease anyone. We are good boys really," James stuttered.

"Good boys! Who among you pulled a girl down onto his lap? You guys trying out some Kama Sutra posture?" He looked from one to the other, like someone following a tennis match from the stands. Ping-Pong, Ping-Pong. When he looked at Johny, James too looked at him. Johny lowered his gaze and the blame was fixed.

"You haven't got a single facial hair and already forcing girls to sit in your lap! I will throw both of you out from this school! Literally, I will catch you guys by the collar, suspend you from my window and drop you on the pavement below." He did hold the two by their collar from behind but did not lift as threatened. In this position he faced their back and they faced Matthias and the wall behind. Indira Gandhi smiled from her photo. James thought in a flash he heard her say "naughty boys" in an approving, likeable mocking reprimand.

"Sir, generally these two are not trouble makers." No, it was not Indira Gandhi speaking for them from the photo on the wall, but their friend Matthias, their guardian angel. "And James here is the topper in Maths and Science. Gets better scores than I do." He said with the humility of a lawyer, presenting a case for the first time to a notorious judge. When it came to diplomacy Matthias had no match and today he was giving it everything he had to get his two buddies out of trouble.

James felt the grip on the collar loosen up. With considerable effort Cherian came around and faced them. "Guys, this is the first and last time you create trouble in my school. One more incident of any sort and I will kick your butts."

As the three boys went out, they heard Cherian mumbling in his non-novelist voice, "What the hell should I tell Catherine, the rollercoaster nasty bum?"

The boys ran out, packed their bags and left the campus. James bought them five rupee chocolates to celebrate their escape. They would celebrate another escape, a couple of years after that, but then beer and Mass wine would replace the chocolates.

4

The Call—Strange are the ways of the Lord

"God calls his favourite sons and daughters to work in his vineyard." The two boys, forced by their parents to attend summer class, sat along with other fifty-odd sixteen year-olds and listened to Father Elias Chakkummoottil roar into the microphone. He loved microphones like a dog loves bones. From a distance one would think he hung on to it with his teeth. His body swayed, his hands gesticulated animatedly but his mouth never moved away from the tip of the microphone. If only he loved his job like he did the reverent instrument.

"He can call you at any time, day or night, in rain or lightning," thundered Father. "But to think that you can be called to the highest vocation possible for a human to achieve—to become a priest in the Holy Catholic Church!" such superlatives made him feel like the most privileged person in the world and he beamed in front of the unfortunate teenagers, who wanted desperately to get out of there. They had completed their stressful 12th standard board examinations, an ordeal by itself, and thought they would be enjoying the holidays until the results came out, but alas that was not to be.

Devout parents thought their boys needed some spiritual awakening and send them to Father Elias' summer camp, of all the places in the world. They would have preferred Siberia.

"Samuel was called in the dead of night! David, when gracing his sheep and Moses in the sight of a burning bush! Where and when he will call . . . it's impossible for us to know. Keep your ears open, boys!" Johny, who was already dosing off, thought the Father had asked him to open his eyes and sat up straight.

The call came three weeks after that, surprisingly to Johny and James. James wanted to get away and Johny thought he had nothing better to do with his poor grades and even poorer family background. At least in Church he would have a decent dwelling, good food and clean clothes. James had the first attack of the 'run-away' complex that would follow him all through his life. This time it had to do with Elena.

James was in tenth grade when he first noticed the shy Elena from Ninth C. She was pretty in a subtle, likeable, girl next door kind of way. She had waist length black hair that curled at the end that was often tied tightly with a hair band or ribbon. Her legs were smooth and shapely, but what drew his attention were her wide, dark eyes that looked at everything with timid curiosity.

For over a week he found opportunities to stare at her from a distance, unseen, in silent admiration. Then he started to visit her class on the pretence of talking to one of his friends who sat in the back row, a neighbour who he had never really acknowledged in the past four years.

He stood near the window and engaged his friend in idle chat about movies and periodicals while staring at his new found interest.

During a very pleasant Friday afternoon break, James had—as usual—slipped away from his two friends and posted himself at the window of Ninth C looking at the petit girl who sat on the second row. She kept talking to another girl, whose back was turned towards James—her big beautiful eyes fluttering and her nimble fingers combing away a few strands of hair that carelessly fell into her face. His heart missed a beat when their eyes met, but it was over in a flash and he couldn't say she had noticed. He could well have been one of the many objects that passed her retina without registering.

Then she looked up again and their eyes met again. He could hear his heart beating, louder than ever before. He moved his gaze to focus on his friend's cream colour uniform shirt but from the corner of his eye he could still see her.

"Hero Pen, Chinese," James' neighbour had proudly pulled out his new fountain pen from the breast pocket of his shirt, thinking James had been staring at it.

"Oh! Good. Very good," he said still in trance.

A bell rang, indicating the end of the break. He ran to his classroom.

He wanted to find out who she was without letting his friends know he was curious about her. If he asked his friends any question about the girl they would get suspicious and start crafting stories about the reason behind his interest. He finally decided to just ask his neighbour, since he was not intimate enough with James to look through his curiosity and see his innermost yearnings.

"Oh, that one? Her name's Elena. She comes every day by bus."

Elena. James thought. Her name indicated she was also a Christian—so there would be no problem concerning their religion.

On the following days James learnt more about her, always asking his neighbour and never too many questions at once, so that no suspicion was raised. Her parents were middle class farmers and though he belonged to the upper middle class he did not see that as a hurdle. They were Syrian Christians migrated to Calicut from Thodupuzha, in Central Kerala. She had one younger brother in Seventh grade and she came everyday by the 9 AM KSRTC bus—he made a clear note of the time.

During this research period, their eyes had met a couple more times. He was glad trying to convince himself that each time the look lasted longer than the time before, but felt sad that those pretty eyes never showed any sign of recognition. Even if you saw a mango tree every day, you might start recognizing it.

James thought she would know him. He was good in studies and stood first in most subjects, except languages and history. He was captain of the school football team, had won medals at state level for two hundred metres sprint for two years and was a close friend of the school secretary. Though not exceptionally good looking or tall like Matthias, he was still decent looking, with a wiry athletic physique and tall for his age. He was offended that an ordinary girl had not heard of him.

It was a leisurely Saturday afternoon. Matthias was directing a skit that would be staged in a couple of weeks, for the school silver jubilee. Johny and James had excused themselves from home to assist their friend and the actors with their rehearsals. They were given official titles such as 'production manager' and 'sound engineer'. They didn't really have anything to do but each boy had their own reason to attend the rehearsals.

Due to a high profile political death and the subsequent weeklong mourning, teachers were trying to catch up with the assigned syllabus for the term, so some of them held special classes on Saturdays. James was pleasantly surprised when he found that Ninth C students were in school that day. With only a few students in school and him being free to roam around, he could dedicate a longer time today to look at Elena. The only difficulty was that he had to stay clear of scary Christina Madam, who arranged the special class for mathematics.

After lunch he had gone to relieve himself in a lonely spot by the mango grove and was strolling back alone, when he saw Elena coming towards him with another girl. They chatted in low voices. He hoped that they did not see him peeing in the open. It was a luxury possible only on Saturdays. On weekdays, boys and girls were supposed to use only the stinking, disgusting, unclean urinals that had all types of amateur drawings and expletives written on its walls.

He became very conscious of himself, the way he walked, where he looked and every part of his body. He saw the other girl elbowing Elena before giggling. He then took courage, thought of his guardian angel—not Matthias but his real one—and looked straight at her. She returned the look with her lovely, dark eyes that spoke more words than he could every say.

"Hi Elena," his left hand was in his pants' pocket and the right one fidgeted with his shirt button.

"Hi" She replied in a very low voice.

"James Mathew, Ten B."

"I know." She said demurely.

"Special Class?"

She nodded.

"Had your lunch?"

She nodded.

"Chocolates?" he pulled out one from his pocket. Go to hell Johny! No chocolates for you today.

She took it.

"And one for your friend" but he gave it to Elena. Sorry Matthias.

"Why are you in school today?" Elena asked. This was the first time his girl was asking him a question.

"Rehearsals. I am the production manager for the skit being staged for the Silver Jubilee celebrations." he said proudly. He wished he knew the connotation of this nomenclature.

Luckily for him, she did not ask any more questions about that subject, only smiled and said "goodbye", waving her hand and looking into his eyes. He closed his eyes when the two girls walked away from him. James pumped his fist in air, "Yes!"

5

You shall sow, I shall reap

It was not easy or socially acceptable for boys and girls in small towns in mid-eighties to meet or spend time together, especially alone. If a boy and girl stood for five minutes chatting under a tree, in an isolated classroom, a lonely path or any such places suitable for romantic exchanges, tongues would wag. Scribbling would soon appear on walls of the classrooms and urinals announcing the couple.

He liked how the names James and Elena looked together and even wrote it many times on a scrap of paper which he later tore into pieces. But he feared the consequences if the same appeared in any other place. Smiles, expressive glances and casual conversations were all that could pass between the two of them, but that left him wanting more.

When desperation began to build up, he decided to confide in his two best friends. The duo was as excited as if they themselves were in love, they felt goose bumps and expressed their surprise that any girl would choose him over either of them.

Urged by movies and serialized novels that were popular at the time, they insisted that he should write her a love letter. Ardent lovers found solace in letters passed through library books, common confidants and placed in agreed hiding places.

Matthias actually wrote the first love letter, as James felt he lacked the literary flair that his friend had in abundance. He was pleasantly surprised at how well the yearnings of his heart had been translated to prose by Matthias after two days of intense sessions. He re-wrote it in his own handwriting and placed it in a copy of Shakespeare's *Romeo and Juliet* that he had picked up from the school library.

"I just finished this book and it's very nice to read. I think you'll find page number twenty six absolutely exciting," He had emphasized while passing the book to her in the school corridor, some of her friends watching. The book was returned the very next day, "I liked the part you recommended but found page eighteen much more interesting."

James had a lump in his throat when he read the first love letter from his girl. He feared his heart would jump out of his mouth and swallowed hard to keep it in its rightful place. For the first time he started admiring his own unkempt hair, his muscular arms, his long shapely nose, his well-set teeth—and whatever other anatomical parts had a favourable reference in Elena's letter. His two friends had looked at him thoughtfully, singling out those parts and trying to figure out why anyone could find them romantic enough to include in a love letter. They were disappointed that there were no hugs and kisses in the letter. They thought these types of letters were always signed off that way.

And they were not disappointed. After a few letters were exchanged between Elena and James, she did send him 'love and kisses' at the closing. James had actually kissed her name below when he first read it yet with his friends he pretended to be composed.

James' mother had an older cousin of hers, Annamma Kunjamma, staying close to where Elena lived. In the past, she had repeatedly requested her son to visit the old aunt and her ailing husband but he had always found excuses. Annamma Kunjamma's two sons had migrated to Ireland and Australia, having married nurses who were employed in those countries. Kunjamma boasted about her sons and James hated her unending chatter.

He knew that Kunjamma's sons were home makers in those countries, mostly baby-sitting while their wives went to work—changing diapers, cleaning utensils, vacuum cleaning the floor and cooking. Servants were more expensive than husbands.

His mother, oblivious to his ploy to meet Elena, was delighted that Sunday when James volunteered to pay a visit to Annamma Kunjamma. He told mother that he would go to the Church near Kunjamma's place at nine in the morning, attend the Mass and then walk down to her house.

He spotted Elena in the Church. She did not see him. She had no reasons to expect him since he belonged to another parish and attended the Church near school. She was very beautiful in her colourful skirt and embroidered beige top. James had always seen her in her uniform as they had always met in school. She was an angel against the backdrop of the church as she stood near the choir, her eyes fixed at the altar. A divine line of tall candles shined at the altar as if ready for procession.

As the final hymn was sung James quietly slipped out of the Church and took position near the gate so that he will not miss Elena as she walks out. He looked smart in a white cotton shirt and dark blue jeans.

He saw mostly men moving out fast, most of them rushing to the nearest beef store to ensure the meat do not run out of stock. Most migrated Catholics bought buffalo meat on Sundays and the butcher would exhibit the animal on Saturday evening to ensure that there is enough rush on Sunday morning. Syrian beef fry is the culinary speciality of the Syrian Catholic Christians of Kerala.

All his enthusiasm suddenly evaporated when James saw Elena walking out with her mother, a lady in her late forties. Elena almost gave a gasp when she saw James at the gate.

"I want to meet with Roshna and Lisa. I will catch up with you," Elena told her mother and walked towards a group of girls who stood chatting under a mango tree while her mother continued walking.

James hung around trying to not to appear staring at her. Elena came near the gate in five minutes but did not stop to greet him. She smiled at James and walked towards the lane leading to her house which stood more than a kilometre away from the Church. James looked around for some time and followed her at a distance. As he reached far enough from the view of the church and the road was lonely enough, he sensed Elena's pace had slowed and his increased.

"Where are you going?" She asked anxiously fearing he would follow her home.

"I came to see you," he lied.

"What? You're mad. Go back. Someone will see," she pleaded. At the same time she was elated that he came all the way to see her.

"You look so beautiful in this dress. They should allow colour dress in school," James said as he walked slowly by her side.

"I am happy you came. I cannot tell you how surprised I am. But I am scared. Please go back and we will meet at school," she tried to convince him.

"Hey, I am actually going to meet my aunt Annamma Kunjamma who lives along the same road," he said.

"Oh, so you did not come to meet me?" she feigned offended.

"My mother has been asking me for a while to go there but now I found a reason," he smiled. She giggled.

She was now comfortable. She had a reason to tell her parents if they were to question her about walking along with a boy all the way from Church.

"She actually lives just two houses away from ours," said Elena.

The more he looked at her eyes, the more he wanted her to be only his. She felt shy when she noticed him looking so intently at her but he did not take his eyes off her.

"The first time I saw you, there was something in your eyes that I liked," he said.

She blushed and looked down.

"I don't know why I feel so much excited when I see you," James kept talking. If someone had to see them then, it was so easy to guess that these two were in love. Luckily no one passed by.

Elena was more forthcoming in her letters but when in person, she spoke little, asked questions and listened to James. If it was a movie, thought James, it was perfect setting for a romantic song. Surrounded by dark green foliage, coffee plantations, nutmeg and jackfruit trees and a pleasant breeze playing naughty with her long hair, there was love in the air.

He said good bye to her as they reached Elena's house. There was no one outside her house and she looked back at him as she entered the house. He felt like rushing to her and hugging her but better sense prevailed. James continued his walk to Annamma Kunjamma's house. He was better prepared today to listen to her banter. After all he could just let his mind wander about Elena when Kunjamma launched her unbearable boasting parade.

On his way back he kept looking at Elena's house if he could at least see her from a distance. He felt an intense yearning to be near her and look into her beautiful eyes. Luck did not favour him this time and he saw her father was watering the plants in the courtyard. James quickened his pace and continued his walk a bit disappointed.

Monday at school he met her in the library and she passed him a sheet of paper. Under the quiet shade of a banyan tree behind the school, he read her love letter. Strange ways of girls, he thought.

She had poured out her heart in each of the lines but she was so silent while they were together just yesterday. She even said that she wanted to hug him when he said good bye but wouldn't dare doing it. James let out a deep sigh. Then he wrote her a letter, all by himself—this time not being conscious of the censure of his friends. And for the first time, he wrote those words and tears came into his eyes when he looked at it again—'I Love you. Only you. Yours only, James'.

Her replay came the next day reciprocating. James was not surprised at her response but what touched him was a beautiful line at the end of the letter, "I cried reading your letter, I must have read it at least 10 times but I just cannot help my eyes filling up each time. It's just too much for me."

There was not a day when they at least didn't look at each other. His every waking moment was filled with her thoughts and when sleeping he dreamt of her. This 'love' thing was crazy and painful.

Despite the fear of getting noticed, James and Elena managed to meet occasionally, creating opportunity to exchange love letters in the humdrum of St Margaret High School.

It was his suggestion that they go for a movie together.

"What? We will be killed! Someone will find out," She was dead scared.

"We will go to a Theatre in Perunthalmanna. People will not know us there," he had planned it out.

I want to be with you but," she paused.

"Nothing will happen. Tell your parents you have a special class on Saturday. We meet at nine and take a bus to the movie. You can get in from your place and I will join from this bus stop," he laid it out.

"I am really scared, James," she looked at him with her wide eyes.

"I will take care that nothing happens," he said. She could sense a special kind of assurance in his voice and his look. There was no wavering or timidity of a teenager in his eyes but confidence and determination of a man.

When he waited for the bus on that Saturday, he knew she would come. There still was an iota of chance that her parents had found out if she could not tell a lie effectively. He found her sitting at the window seat of the nine O'clock KSRTC. The bus was relatively free and he took another seat from where he could see her.

They had ice cream in a small ice cream parlour on reaching Perinthalmanna. She was silent in the beginning but then started talking about how she managed to get away that morning.

"It is good that my father is not in the habit of coming to our school or talking to any of the teachers. Otherwise, he would have known that there was no special class today," she cautioned.

"There is a long line for the show," he was the first to get up.

"No worries. The lady's line is a short one. I will buy the tickets," she offered.

"Smart!" he smiled as he handed her the money. "Balcony."

Less than ten minutes, she was back with two Pink colour tickets for balcony. There were three classes, Balcony, Yellow circle and Green Circle. Balcony had more privacy being at the back, with only few rows of push back seats and stood elevated from the eyes of other classes below.

Slowly, one by one, the lights were off and the screen lit up. After a few news reels that spoke of agriculture and tobacco, the censor certificate of the movie was displayed. Even colourful movies had dull, tastelessly designed censor board certificates.

It was a sentimentally charged love story with some crazy twists and a sad ending. James did not concentrate on the movie at all. He kept looking at Elena as the flashes from the screen reflected on her cheeks. She too was less aware of the movie than his presence next to her. This was the first time; they were sitting so close together, that too in darkness. In a careful act of carelessness he touched her arms with his. One touch and quick pull back. She too pulled her hand back. Next moment her hand was back on the hand rest. This time he kept his hand next to hers their skin touching. She did not pull back.

He remained in that position for about five minutes and he could feel a warmth and softness he has never before experienced. Then he could not hold it any longer and he held her hand. She let him and looked at him. He wanted to kiss her in darkness but a fat man sitting behind them coughed aloud and cleared his throat scaring James in the process. He sat tight, still holding her arms and gently fondling her fingers.

When the lights came on and credits were still scrolling up the screen, James and Elena woke up from their two hours of intimacy and quickly moved out. They got into the first bus drawing an end to one of the most memorable days in their budding romance.

It slowly grew into a tree in the following months—watered abundantly by a torrent of love letters, stealthy meetings and occasional escapades.

James had not drifted away from his friends Matthias and Johny though much of their share in his mind had been given away for Elena. The two were regularly updated about the developments in his adventures making the two happy and jealous at the same time.

As the secretary of students committee, Matthias got himself busy with the annual cultural meet. The students were divided into four houses and had competed in twenty-five cultural events. The houses have always been named unimaginatively, Red, Blue, Green and Yellow. The events, rules and regulations, judges and venues had to be finalised. He had pulled in James and Johny to help him as both of had no inclination for any cultural competitions. James was in charge of co-ordinating with judges—mostly teachers.

Mr Unnikrishnan, a talented singer who was the staff member in charge of the cultural festival, suggested that a small group of girls should also be part of the core organising committee for better interaction with girl students. Most girls would be reluctant to talk to boys as organisers. This was music to the ears of Johny and Matthias.

However, the choice of girl students was left to some of the class teachers. It was one of the Malayalam teachers who was also the class teacher for Nine C who nominated Elena.

James could not believe his eyes when he walked into the core committee meeting next morning and saw Elena and two other girls were engaged in serious discussion with Matthias. In any such meetings, it was very clear that Matthias was in charge.

"Friends, let me introduce to you the new members of the organising committee," Matthias formally introduced the three girls while James continued to stand there with open mouth. Elena only smiled. She knew James was part of the committee and had hoped to meet him there.

Though committee meetings in the following days gave him an opportunity to be with Elena legitimately, their nature of work required them to work separately. James had hoped that Matthias would club them together but his friend was too focused on the task at hand to give heed to such sentiments. For Matthias, successful conducting of the event was far more important to fostering his friend's romance. Such favouritism would only ruin the team work.

Elena was given the charge of enrolling participants from the girls' side while James was mostly running after the teachers trying to sign them up as judges. Shy and reluctant by nature, Elena had to be mentored and encouraged to reach out to girls across different houses and ensure that there were enough participation from girls. Matthias guided her at every step, hand holding her at meetings, correcting when going wrong and boosting her morale when she failed.

Elena, like most students in junior classes, had only admired Matthias from a distance but now she was working closely with him. She soon realised that his popularity and glamour did not come without a reason. He was distinctively focused; intelligent, cool and composed even when things did not go well. Adding to all this was his tall and handsome personality and disarming smile.

Matthias had also accompanied her to some of the meetings that she had with groups of girls. When he was around she felt more confident.

Some of the girls in Elena's class were the first to tease her about her closeness to the most desirable boy in school. Only then did she realise that she had been too frequently seen with him and since the reasons for their interactions were perfectly rational, there was no effort from either of them to be discreet.

There were many girls whose main hobby was to spin yarn at the slightest opportunity. Soon among such population the possible romance between Elena and Matthias did its spicy rounds.

There was another reason why many believed that there was fire behind the smoke. Elena did not deny the story with the expected vehemence when confronted by some of her own classmates. She thought it would probably hide her relationship with James.

James was the first boy that she had ever interacted so closely and Matthias the second. She had never thought that she could ever like someone the way she did these two. She loved James and his passionate love for her was so overwhelming to her. On the other hand, she leaned on Matthias, admired him and genuinely looked forward to his company.

Annual cultural fest was a huge success, even Cherian Kora, admitting it as one of the best conducted events in the recent years. There were loud applauses when Matthias was called on stage at the concluding function. He then called his team and thanked them mentioning their contribution. For Elena it was her first time on stage—that too cheered by the entire student community. Matthias had cheered her on stage announcing that if it was not for Elena, record participation from the girls would not have been possible. She felt so conscious of such attention and some of her classmates whistled from the back row.

Even after the cultural fest Elena found time to meet Matthias often to take his guidance in study related matters. Matthias, who had now turned his attention to studies, did find time to pay her attention whenever she approached him.

Matthias knew all about her relationship with James but never dragged that matter into their discussion. She too never volunteered to discuss her romance with him. Nor did she mention of the rumour linking Matthias and her.

James could not recollect exactly when, but towards the second half of the 12th grade, he got this strange idea that Elena was taking him for granted and showing more interest in being with some of his friends, particularly Matthias. In the beginning he had ignored her closeness to Matthias because anyone close to James would invariably be friends with his best friend.

"Have you heard the latest story?" asked James' neighbour who studied in Elena's class one day.

"What story?" James was confused.

"About that girl you once asked details about, Elena"

"What about her," James was curious now.

"Looks like she is in love with Matthias," said the neighbour. James felt a lightning passing within his chest.

"Nonsense!" he looked away. "You know Matthias and I are friends. This cannot be true!"

"Maybe. Yet, the rumour is pretty strong, especially among girls." He said and walked away.

James sat down on a stone and shook his head. What's going on? He did not know whether to laugh or to cry.

He could see visible changes in Elena's behaviour when she started meeting Matthias more frequently.

"You seem to be really busy these days," said James when he met her after two days. "I was looking for you last evening."

"There was a meeting of class representatives," she said. Following her active participation in various organising committees encouraged and mentored by Matthias, she was now the class representative. She was so unnoticed and shy when James had discovered her but now she was behind every major event in the school.

"There was a long list of recommendations that had to be discussed with headmaster. There are as many opinions as people and absolutely no consensus," she was animated.

"Oh," James just kept looking at her.

"Then walks in Matthias and gets absolute control of the discussions. Within half an hour there was a consensus and a list with priority ratings alongside," she said.

"He has a nice way of influencing people," James said.

"He is too smart, no?" she said thoughtfully.

Why she is asking me, thought James.

"I was really scared the way some of the class representatives were agitated over the cleanliness of toilets. Some even said we should go on strike," she continued not waiting for his response.

"Benny suggested we throw stones at Cherian Kora's car," Benny was the younger brother of local CITU leader, Sojan. James knew him and his propensity to jump into conflicts.

"The way Matthias handled him was just awesome," she beamed as if she had won over the chaos. James felt uneasy.

This was not the last time she would sing the school secretary's praises. If it was with reference to dealing with a teacher one day, it was about how well he spoke at a function another day.

James was kind of feeling distanced when she launched such litany.

He also noticed that over time, his relationship was taken for granted. As if he would be there anyway. She did not find new ways of surprising him like they did in the past three years. Letters had become infrequent, not because of Elena but he had found the novelty wearing away.

Within him he knew well that Matthias was way far the best guy in school and most desirable for any girl. If Elena was enjoying Matthias' company and if she nurtures such admiration for him, you could not blame her. James' agony was that he wanted her to be only his. Now he doubted it.

He tried to put up a show of indifference towards her for a few days and felt miserable when she did not notice it.

He could usually discuss all his problems with his two friends but this was a case where he could not share his burden with them. Not even once did Matthias bring up the topic with him and instead, seemed to encourage Elena, going out of his way to accommodate her.

Board examinations were fast approaching and James hid himself in preparations and filled his mind with academic jargon to get over his obsession with Elena.

He started telling himself why Matthias was a better fit for her than himself. Matthias was exceptionally handsome, just out of a Bollywood movie, he also had a remarkable gift of gab when on stage or during one-on-one interactions. He was a guy any teenage girl would die for.

James even contemplated the idea that Elena had become friendly with him only to get closer to Matthias, who was admired by everyone in school. He felt like a piece of shit and turned vehemently to his studies, avoiding interaction with Elena in the attempt to subdue his aching heart.

School study leave provided an opportunity not to meet her for a whole month. He confined himself to his house, ate little, read books, slept inadequately and avoided calling her. He felt his doubts and fears had been confirmed when he did not get any calls from her. He even avoided spending much time with his friends during the break.

The examinations were over in fifteen days. He found them easy compared to the much tougher test he was facing in his love life. Immediately after the school was closed, Matthias went off to Muscat along with his parents to spend the holidays with one of his uncle's family. He had called James once, speaking about the fun he was having with his cousins and some of the wonderful places he visited.

James had buried himself in a pile of tragedy novels he had picked up from his father's collection and felt even more miserable. He wondered whether his father had ever had his heart broken, to justify such an enormous collection of depressing novels.

That is when "the Call" came, in the form of a phone call from Fr. Elias to James' father, Mathew Pulikkan. Fr. Elias was holding a three days camp on vocation to priesthood and wanted all Catholic young men, who had completed their 12th grade, to attend. "The harvest is full, but labourers are few," church Father quoted and boy's father nodded. In sorrow and confusion he decided to check out the priestly vocation, denouncing his first love and responding to the Lord's call.

"The Call" came to Johny almost biblically. Fr. Elias was on his way to administer the anointing of the sick to an old lady who lived far away from the Church. The road to the house was steep and filled with a narrow and rocky terrain, so that Father had to abandon his old Ambassador car almost a kilometre down the hill and continue his sacramental journey uphill by foot.

He was tired and the summer heat made beads of sweat shine like pearls on his bald head. He stopped in the middle of the way to steady his breathing and saw Johny's house. He wanted to have some cold water or butter milk to quench his thirst, and take the opportunity to give some free advice to Johny's father, who was a renowned drunkard in this parish. Finding no one in the house he was about to return to the road, disappointed at not having his buttermilk, when suddenly something like a nut fell on his slippery bald scalp, glided off slimly and landed on the floor. It was a jack nut! He crossed himself and thanked the Lord that it was just a nut, and not a jackfruit.

Looking up he saw Johny perched on the branch of a jackfruit tree, happily feasting on a ripe fruit, oblivious to the presence of the man of God below. "Johny, come down!" he called out.

Johny was startled and almost fell off the branch. The jackfruit slipped and came down, splashing against the pavement. Father again crossed himself and thanked the Lord that it landed a good three feet away from his reverent head. The Lord had saved him twice in a short span of minutes.

The boy climbed down quickly, apologizing all the way while Father Elias busied himself with picking out a few pieces that had splashed on his white cassock.

"Johny, I want to have some buttermilk at your home." He said and remembered the Lord offering to dine at the tax collector Zacchaeus' house. If the Lord could have dinner at a tax collector's house, why shouldn't he have some buttermilk at a drunkard's hut?

Johny ran inside and came out with a tall steel tumbler of buttermilk. That cooled the agitated clergy and his cool head spun with new ideas.

"Johny," said Father. "You should come and attend the vocation camp starting next Monday. Who knows how and when God calls? I have had the privilege of taking the Lord's call to many young priests, if I may say so." He took pride in being the embodiment of humility. Johny knew it was not a suggestion but an order and showed up on Monday, ten minutes late, to show his protest against being dragged into the camp.

But he soon started liking it because the food was free, and good, and James was there as well. The first two days were utterly boring to the boys. Father Elias in his usual eloquence went on and on about priestly vocation. There was a nun too, Sister Thereasa who conducted a group discussion on 'why you want to be a priest'. It ended up a monologue where the Sister was the only speaker while the boys kept mum.

Towards the end of second day the boys were relieved to meet a new face, who Father Elias introduced as being that of Father Aloysius Pius, the diocesan 'vocation promoter'. He was a young and dynamic priest who moved from parish to parish, conducting sessions at vocation camps and recruiting future priests for the diocese.

"Young men," Fr. Aloysius addressed the boys. They felt better for the automatic upgrade in their status. So far everyone called them 'boys'.

"Are you all enjoying the camp?"

The boys looked around and finding that Father Elias was not around shook their head in negation.

"Then let's have some fun," he said. Boys looked at one another in puzzlement.

"Let us all stand up," he rolled up his sleeve.

There was a hum of whispers and shuffle of feet and the boys stood up.

"Move all the chairs close to the wall and form a circle in the middle of the hall" the boys followed the direction. Now there was excitement and anticipation.

Fr. Aloysius drew two lines in the middle of the room and divided the boys in two teams.

"The game is simple. The two lines indicate the shores of a river and the team that crosses the river faster with maximum members will win the game. I will time it on my stopwatch." He outlined. The boys thought it a cakewalk.

"Now the rules. The river is infested by dangerous crocodiles. The only way to keep them off is to hold this magic towel," he exhibited a white handkerchief.

"If you tie this on your wrist, crocodile cannot attack you," he said.

The width of the river was too much for someone to jump across or throw the handkerchief back.

"Can we use a stone to throw the handkerchief back?" asked Johny.

"No you cannot use any other properties. You can through the handkerchief itself but it may not make it across and once dropped in the water it loses its magical power," now it was getting tougher.

You get five minutes to plan your strategy after which team A will start. Both the teams had pretty much the same strategy. The strongest person ties the handkerchief on his wrist and lifts other members to cross the river. Half way through the strongest member was absolutely tired, and someone else stepped in.

Some guys stumbled and fell and lost the game. In team B, James almost single handed carried most of the boys across. One fat boy however, got scared and fell into the river.

At the end of it all, the boys were energetic and alert.

They had a short break during which they animatedly discussed about the game.

"Did you enjoy the game?" asked Father.

"Yes!" came the unanimous reply.

"We will have many such games later today," Father promised.

"Now, tell me what you learnt from this game. About you and about working in teams," he asked them once they had re-arranged their chairs and were seated.

This interesting discussion was followed by a very engaging and humorous talk by Father Aloysius. Youngsters, who had almost dozed off during the boring torments of the first forty-eight hours, were now fully alert.

James and Johny thought he was cool and with such people around, the minor seminary did not seem like a bad option. They fell for the young priest's sales pitch and were filling up their application forms the next day. They were being considered for the job of aspiring harvesters of the Lord's vineyard. Of the fifty odd young people attending the camp, five applied, all five were interviewed and after the necessary verifications only two were chosen.

James and Johny went home to announce to their families their decision to join the minor Seminary as Aspirants, from the 13th of the following month.

James' devout parents were ecstatic that their son had been called by God, though they were sorry that he would have to go so soon.

Johny's mother was glad that the poor boy would now get a decent place to stay, a reasonable amount of food on a regular basis and also be spared of his father's drunken episodes. She has never heard of any priest ever dying of hunger. The ones she'd heard about had died because of high cholesterol, high blood pressure, liver cirrhosis or diabetics, diseases mostly associated with the well-fed.

6

The Minor Seminary

The monsoon had struck early over the western coast and it was pouring cats and dogs when James and Johny were dropped at the Minor Seminary. It was formed by an imposing line of buildings that stood in a sprawling fifty acre land, very close to the Kunnamkulam town. There were five buildings varying in shapes and heights but all of them had the same colour—ashen grey with thick blue lines running horizontally, like a huge ribbon tied around a dull gift box. A church stood within the compound to conduct services for the seminarians and was open to the devotees who lived nearby. It was some four kilometres away from the Cathedral and the Archbishop's house.

The boys were received by Fr. Aloysius at the reception, with his customary broad smile and eloquent words of welcome.

"There is nothing like a refreshing rain to welcome you to the Lord's vineyard. These are the showers of blessing," he lifted both his hands to the sky in a dramatic gesture.

After assuring that their wards would be well taken care of and were safe in God's custody, he sent James' father—who had come to drop both boys off—away.

"There are thirty seminarians in this batch, twenty five have already checked in," said the Father as he led them through a long corridor. When they were in school they had been called students for twelve years, now they were a part of new collective noun: seminarians.

"Come, let me take you to your dormitory," he took the stairs followed closely by the two boys, struggling to carry their huge bags. They thought they were packing for life and included all that was required and available—excluding porno books, love letters and painful memories from the past. They were here for good—to become as the book of Psalm says, 'a priest forever in the order of Melchizedek of old'.

The dormitory was a large hall on the 4th floor with four rows of iron coats complete with white bed spreads, pillows and mosquito nets. At the head of each of them was a wooden cupboard with drawers. The hall was well ventilated with many windows. There were several tube lights, several ceiling fans and an iron box plugged to a switchboard.

When they entered there were many boys standing or sitting in groups of fours and fives chatting, but at the sight of the priest they were all stiffened into silence.

"Take it easy young men!" said the Father. "You may freshen up and take some rest. Then you can go assemble at the adjoining study room at half past eleven and I will introduce you to Fr. Philip Kurian, your Master." Father Aloysius retreated.

Most of the early comers had already taken all the preferred spots near the windows with a view, the premium ones facing the public road outside the compound wall. James and Johny found three free slots in a corner and settled for two of them. They went around and introduced themselves and started getting to know the people with whom they would spend the foreseeable future.

At eleven thirty, when all the new seminarians assembled in the study room, they were twenty nine of them. Thirty boys alone in a classroom would have toppled the roof, but here, everyone sat in near silence save some whispers and new introductions. Most of them wore pants and full sleeved shirts. James felt like he was in a straightjacket. There was a desk for each; and on top of them, a couple of notebooks, some pencils, an eraser and a pen. James and Johny managed to occupy one of the rows in the back, next to each other.

There was pin drop silence when they heard the shuffle of polyester cassocks followed by the grand entry of Father Aloysius and a grumpy looking fat priest in late forties—with salt and pepper beard and oily thinning hair. He entered stomach first, body later, and slumped into the chair behind the table facing the boys while his younger colleague stood smiling disarmingly, like a sales man who has clinched a multimillion-dollar deal.

"Dear seminarians, I am happy to introduce to you Fr. Philip Kurien, the Master of Aspirants. He is one of the most senior members of this community and has been in this role for the past four years," then, in a graceful and dramatic motion towards Father Philip he invited, "over to you, Father."

As soon as the senior stood up the vocation promoter was gone and the boys felt scared.

"Starting today, you Aspirants are going to begin your Seminary life. I am your Master," he stopped and let the impact of the word 'Master' sink in. "You are called 'Aspirant' because you aspire to enter the Holy Order of Priesthood. Is there anyone who does not aspire?" he stopped and looked around.

Everyone aspired.

"You will hence forth address each other and the senior Seminarians as 'Brothers'. There are only Fathers and Brothers here. Is that clear?"

It was.

"You will maintain silence in this building except during recreation and sports hours. This is a house of prayer and meditation." Some of the boys drew a deep breath.

"There is a time table published at the notice board behind this classroom and you will always adhere to that to the dot. It starts with the wake up bell at five in the morning."

Sighs again, as the earliest risers among them had never seen the light of day before seven.

"The morning meditation and prayers will begin sharp at six, followed by the Holy Mass. Breakfast is served at half past seven." The boys brightened for the first time as they heard the reference of something to which they would look forward every day.

The Master went on to outline a draconian schedule with occasional silver linings like one hour of sports in the evening and thirty minutes of recreation after dinner. They prayed in the morning, at noon, in the evening and at night. Between the last prayer of the day and breakfast, it was strictly forbidden for anyone to speak—even if the building came crashing down. The rest of the time they had work in all different parts of the building and outside, in the garden.

The vocation promotion and the actual seminary life differed from each other as much as recruitment and employment, embodied by the enchantment of Fr. Aloysius and the strictness of Fr. Philip.

A round of introductions followed, where each one got up and mentioned his name, native village or town and who their favourite saint was. "Baiju Sebastian" said the short and timid boy in the first row.

"Brother Baiju Sebastain!" corrected the Master.

"Brother, Father" the boy stammered.

Fortunately for James and Johny by the time their turn came they had enough time to rehearse their version. John and James were the best options they could think of and for novelty's sake they each choose the other's name for their patron saints.

"May I come in Father?" all heads turned towards the door at the sound of the husky feminine voice that interrupted the series of introductions.

There stood a handsome boy, fair skinned, with wavy smooth hair and bright eyes. He looked scared and almost on the verge of crying.

"What time is it?" asked Father.

"Coming from Nilambur, Father. The bus broke down on the way. I am very sorry Father." Maybe because the whole thing sounded like sitting in the confessional or because he thought the boy would start crying, Father Philip accepted his apology and allowed him in.

"Now, introduce yourself, your native place and your favourite saint. No. Just the name and saint will do, you've already said you came from Nilambur."

The boy was still settling down at the desk next to James when the question came. He stood up holding the table to prevent himself from shivering. Now the table shook with him.

"Zacharia, sir . . . err . . . Father, Zacharia Tharakan" he said.

"Brother Zacharia!" corrected Fr. Philip.

"Father Zacharia . . . sorry. Brother Zacharia, Father."

"And your favourite saint?"

The boy looked down to think of a suitable name . . . "Saint Carl Marx, Father."

"What?" the Father's eyes popped out as if the boy had mentioned Lucifer. But on second thought, he divined that Brother Zacharia was simply scared and ignorant.

"Marx is not a saint, Brother. He was a communist! An atheist."

"Alphonsamma?" asked the boy after a long pause. Now, Blessed Alphosamma—a devout nun who lived at Bharananganam in Kottayam district in the first half of the century—was likely to be made a saint in the near future.

Now it was Father Philip who thought for a while and then said, "Well, I will give it to you. She is not a saint yet but could be made one any day. Now sit down!"

"Now Brothers, please stand up for a short prayer, after which we will proceed to the refectory for lunch." The boys learnt yet another word; they were slowly being inducted into the seminary terms and life.

The prayer was not short as announced by the priest. In his fervent extempore prayer, Father Philip invoked several saints and angels. He pleaded with them to save these new Aspirants from all evil influence, give them strength to guard the virtues of chastity, obedience and poverty, shower abundance of blessings. They thought it had ended with the '*amen*' but he broke into a hymn. At the end of it, when the boys were bored and hungry, he asked them to march in silence towards the refectory on the ground floor.

They reached it two minutes before lunch was served and saw many Brothers and Fathers already assembled, waiting in silence with their eyes glued to the feast on the table. There was rice, chapattis, beef, *dal*, cabbage and pickle. Some of the boys were happy with what they saw, others frowned.

An old priest in grey hair and white cassock walked in and began a short prayer at the end of which the new boys waited to observe and imitate the seniors. To their surprise, the prayer had hardly ended and a bunch of Fathers and senior Brothers had jumped forward picked up the plates and had begun serving themselves generously, some even shoving their competitors.

Too shy to do the same, the Aspirants approached their table meekly, picking up plates without making much noise, and began serving themselves. When his turn came, James found the beef plate empty and when the last guy, Zacharia reached the table, there was only rice, dal and pickles. He sat quietly with James and Johny.

They would soon fashion themselves after the seniors.

In the next few days the boys had some surprises, learned many more do's and don'ts and began their work and classes. They played football, volleyball and basketball in the evenings, depending on what was scheduled.

Along with the Johny, Zaccharia was now mostly seen with James. He was unique among the seminarians. He only spoke with a few, followed the rules to the iota and kept belongings clean and organised. He had delicate features, matching his gait and voice, and during the games his shorts showed off hairless legs. James thought some of the seniors looked at his thighs with hunger in their eyes, but dismissed the thought as being the design of demons.

As he got to know his Brothers better, James found to his great amusement that 'the Call' had come to many of them in strange forms.

Two guys from the hilly terrain had joined the Seminary because their parents could not afford to send them to college. A rich brat from the city was there because his parents had felt that a few years with priests would improve his English language and his morning habits, including cleanliness. Another had joined because his mother had gone through some imagined impending calamity, even before being pregnant with him, and had promised in a vow to Velankanni shrine that her son would become a priest. There was another guy who was generally afraid of girls and had thought that by being in a place like seminary he had a legitimate reason to keep away from them.

There were boys who were smart, pious, disciplined and friendly and there were others who were dumb, crooked, gluttonous and horny but somehow they all found a way to coexist and progressively made friends with the each other.

There were also seniors and priests some of who had landed up due to strange reasons and had grown accustomed to this life, the luxury of not having to work and earn or look after a family, and had resigned to their fate of not having a woman all their life. Some led assiduously chaste and clean lives and worked and prayed hard. Others enjoyed the camaraderie of commune and played to the demands of the majority. Sly among them swindled Church money and emancipated their greedy or poor relatives. A few flirted with women; of these some fell in love and left priesthood in order to marry their lover. Others continued on with their love lives in tandem with priestly life, the truth known only to some harmless souls. The shadows of the sacristy and the boring hours spent working at the barns became the meeting grounds of such forbidden lovers.

Seminary schedule provided for long silent hours and they were initially excruciating for James, who was still haunted by the thought of Elena, her pretty face, her curious-large eyes and her soft voice. He was not sure where she was and made no effort to find out.

Whenever he thought of her something rolled up from his gut and stuck at his throat. While his eyes kept staring blankly at the crucifix or the tabernacle during the meditation time, he felt the whining of his heart, his longing to be near her, hold her hands and ask her to be only his.

One night he was lying along on the terrace looking up at the expanse of the sky when his thoughts were again invaded by Elena.

"Lord, why is this happening to me?" he pleaded. "I have come to be at your service. Why can't I forget the aching of my heart? What should I do?"

He closed his eyes and prayed. Then got up and vowed to keep busy with so much work that he will not be distracted. "You should help me, Lord," he looked up before walking back to his dormitory.

From the next day, whenever he thought of her, he recited a *Hail Mary* for her welfare and got himself busy with various activities that the seminary offered.

7

Spirituality and Intimacy

Father Mark was popular with the Aspirants. He taught them English literature and was very knowledgeable in many subjects, with a Doctorate in Philosophy from some Italian university. His sermons were inspiring, interesting and practical. He was composed while on pulpit and spoke straightforwardly, always with a smile. He was also good at the games and mingled with the boys, to the annoyance of Father Emil, the rector of the seminary.

Father Emil, who was in his late fifties, has been the head of the minor seminary for five years and was known for having a commanding personality and the sternness of a dictator. He lived an unstained and disciplined life, never mingled freely with the Brothers or Sisters in the convents. Always one of the first to rise, he did his morning walks with his rosary beads moving between his fingers. He prayed for a long time sometimes alone, sometimes with others in the Chapel, was on time for all his assignments, whether teaching or praying or eating. Father Emil ate frugally and abstained from eating meat, except on Sundays. There was a rumour that he washed his hands twenty times a day using Pears soap. This was his only indulgence, purity and cleanliness. He was not happy that some of the priests, like Mark, came in physical contact with the boys, held their hands, collided with them in the basketball court and even put their hand around the shoulders.

James thought of Father Mark as being a good friend and guide, and requested him to be his spiritual director. Not only the Aspirants but all seminarians under formation were required to have a spiritual director apart from their Master. It was with him that you discussed the progress of your vocation and received guidance of how to grow closer to God.

Mark and James shared a passion for good books, both being voracious readers, though each had his unique preference. James was fond of Victorian writers and twentieth century American writers. Father Aloysius read most Indian English writers and leading Malayalam novels and travelogues. He also introduced James to the reading of Christian and non-christian philosophers. It was not easy to digest Immanual Kant or Thomas Aquinas initially but with his spiritual director's help, he started understanding them. Loke, Home and Spencer were read and discussed as were Comte, Sartre and Camus before starting off with Indian philosophers like Adi Sankara and Aurobindo.

With Mark's encouragement, and to James' own surprise, he began to consider becoming a priest for the sake of serving God and his people, and not in order to avoid an ex-girlfriend.

Of all his thirty-something friends, he was closest to Johny and Zach. In their own different ways, they both complemented him. While James was intelligent, studied hard and excelled in sports, Johny was lazy in his studies and games but made up for it with practical shrewdness; he had a penchant for mischief at every opportunity. James was macho and more strongly built than most others in the batch, while Zach was quiet and fragile, almost feminine.

Despite of being initially irritated with Zach's dependence on him, James started liking the other boy's presence and was becoming attached to him. At times, Zach reminded him of Elena in the early days of their relationship. He enjoyed the physical closeness, holding hands as they went for their Sunday walks in the nearby park or strolling among the casuarina trees within the lonely parts of the vast seminary compound. Two of the things that they had in common were their liking for each other's company and having Fr. Mark as their spiritual director.

Though most of the days went in monotonous series of work, prayer and classes, there were a few days in the year that all the seminarians looked forward to. Special feast days and anniversaries were celebrated with splendour, the highlight being sumptuous lunches and dinners. Annual cultural and sports meet was another exciting time with the entire seminary being grouped into four teams and intense spirit of competition and teamwork at display. While James ended up as part of the organising team, Johny was busy fixing matches and ran a miniature betting program. Zach participated in some written events with not much success except for a third place in poetry writing.

The most eventful of all was the Picnic day. Plans and preparations began much in advance. Wynad was finalised as the location and committees were formed for food, entertainment and transportation. Entertainment committee chalked out the games and music and created parody songs to keep the fun quotient. Food committee decided on the menu and was responsible to join the cooks the previous night to prepare and pack the breakfast and lunch. The dinner would be eaten from a local restaurant.

A fifty seat bus was booked and the team started off early in the morning. There were three priests accompanying the boys, Fathers Philip, Mark and Aloysius. There was much silence initially, and then, Father Philip initiated a prayer song and everyone joined in.

"Boys, this is a picnic and not a 'way-of-the-cross'," Announced Father Aloysius now standing in the front row facing everyone.

"Can I hear three cheers? Hip-hip-hurray!," he screamed and all repeated. "Three cheers for Father Philip, please!" The boys cheered.

"Now we will have a parody song from the entertainment committee," announced Father Aloysius. Four guys took out their notes and sang a song that made fun of everyone including the Fathers present and about various aspects of seminary life. Fathers Mark and Aloysius cheered them and repeated the lines after them. Peppy music, dance and housie games followed this live entertainment all the way to Wynad.

The whole day was exciting. They had enthusiastically trekked to Edakkal caves, crawled their way down to Soojippara falls and played in the fresh waters in Kuruva Island and wondered looking down from the Viewpoint at the ninth bend. More than the places of attraction the boys enjoyed the spirit of being together in an informal setting. At some point even Father Philip shed his seriousness and was running like a pumpkin on the cricket ground, dropping catches and diving near the boundary.

After a sumptuous dinner at a Muslim restaurant in Vythiri, they boarded their bus, tired but happy. It was half past ten and the first two kilometres saw many of them dosing off.

As the tourist bus began its long winding journey downhill, the young men were already slumbering in the comfort of their push back seats, their face caressed by the cool breeze. They felt great after a hectic picnic and a daylong visit to many interesting spots in the hill district.

They had loved the fog hugging hills from each of these bends in the morning but now it was dark all around, save for the headlights of the occasional trucks that snailed their way up the road.

James was suddenly nostalgic; this environment reminded him of his hometown and of Elena. He cursed himself for not having forgotten her already. Zach sat next to him, napping off like a baby with a beige fluffy shawl around him, and Johny was in the seat behind them. There was a chill in the air and James felt foolish for not having brought anything to keep himself warm.

Zach, even though being in half stupor, offered to share his shawl with James. The shawl was big enough to cover the two of them and the warmness they felt from each other's body inside the soft wool was comforting.

They held their hands and slowly dozed off to the warm bosom of slumber. Half an hour must have passed when James jerked his head up to find Zach's head on his shoulder, his soft cheeks resting on James' muscles as he slept like a child. Their hands were still clasped together.

Zach's arms were smooth, warm and felt like velvet against James' sinewy, hairy arm. Cuddling, they slept through the hairpin bends, oblivious of the dark and deep cliff that held stories of many fatal falls. In the clouds, James saw himself and Elena, in a sweet long embrace as the warm morning sun wrapped them with its bright warmth. He kissed her burning hot lips with passion, and she opened them in total submission and fervour. They could feel the pounding of each other's heart and feel the ache of passion. And then they slept.

James sat in the chapel alone with the bible open in his lap and his eyes resting on the large rosewood crucifix on the wall. He had been there for nearly an hour, trying to find out why he was feeling that way. He was here to ask the Lord what he wanted of him, His eager servant. And the Lord seemed to ignore him. If He wanted me why let me feel this way? James found the silence agonising.

He closed the bible, rushed to the dormitory, changed into his shorts and jersey and went to join his friends in the basketball court. He played vigorously until he was drenched in sweat and it felt good enough to make him feel normal. He tried not to be alone again that day and joined in whenever a large number of guys gathered. He felt much better.

As months and years passed contradictions between what was believed and practiced bubbled up in the minds of the seminarians. The Lord of the poor who felt their hunger and pain, prayed for them and taught them to love one another was enshrined in the scriptures. He was a rebel in his own community and was hung from a cross till he bled to his death. His early followers too lived in poverty, sharing what they had and dying for the faith.

The young men, who were fast growing out of their teens, were initially amazed at the hypocrisy of some of the clergymen. They almost fitted exactly into the Lord's own description of the Pharisees and priests of the Jews—whitewashed sepulchres! While on pulpit they preached love and forgiveness. In life they loathed their fellowmen, schemed against their own kind and fought for positions of power. They taught the scriptures that they did not practice. A small number of aspirants walked out, unable to bear the psychological dissonance that overpowered them.

"What you believe is what you practice, not what you denounce," one boy had lamented before walking away.

For many others, nothing seemed weird or sacrilegious and they found a way to live with the contradictions between their beliefs and practices, in a kind of hypocritical bliss. They formed their own philosophy of life and designed their own God.

They believed in their right to mould His image according to their liking—and gosh, did they feel good about their creativity! Some talked of faith; some of charity and others of love—all manifestations of God. They read books, wrote theses and debated these various manifestations and felt haughty about it all. And they did what they pleased, conniving against others, scheming for power, over eating and rumour mongering.

Johny had, by now, made a name for himself among his batch mates and seniors as a dependable man. He was the first to smuggle in a 'matter' video into the seminary. He had learned from one of the seniors that a certain priest used to hire porn movies from a local video parlour. Gathering up courage, Johny had walked to the shop keeper and introduced himself as a close friend of the wayward priest and said he was earnestly referred by his friend to what he considered to be the best video parlour in town. In a few minutes he was out of the parlour with a smart collection of triple X and soft porn videocassettes.

The show was scheduled for after mid-night, when everyone that didn't matter was asleep. Only those who, according to Johny, could keep their mouths and zippers closed were invited. They took bed sheets, towels and newspapers with them to cover the window panes, so that the flicker from the TV monitor would not be detected by anyone outside. In the cemetery-like silence of darkness, the future Fathers and Brothers watched—open mouthed—the coarsest ways of lovemaking.

James attended some of the initial showings but stopped, for fear of getting caught, when some of the seniors started getting over excited, shouting crude expletives while encouraging the screen couple. Zach was neither invited nor interested.

Once, as James tip-toed back to the dormitory, leaving one of the shows half way through, he passed close to Fr. Mark's room and found that the light in the room was still on. He wondered how long the Father stayed awake, and how he could look so fresh and rested at six in the morning if he went to bed this late. He was about to resume his journey to bed when he heard someone's whisper coming from the direction of the dimly lit room. Did Father Mark call his family after midnight to save on the STD tariff? That wasn't very likely, as telephone bills were paid by the office. Plus, why should any relatives keep awake till one or two in the morning to receive a call?

He blamed Satan for arousing in his mind the idea that Father Mark had some woman in his room, but it did seem like a possible explanation. On the one side, the

Father had an impeccable history and no woman could get this far into the compound without someone seeing her. Instead of walking back to his dormitory, he kicked off his floaters and walked, quiet as a cat, approaching the door with each careful step. The whispers had stopped but he could hear faint movements from inside. He tried looking through the keyhole but couldn't see anything. The corridor was dark because one of the tube lights had fused off. James found a stool at the end of the corridor, placed it next to the window and, stretching on his toes, peeped through pane.

He saw Father Mark's back, sweaty muscles in dim light. He was hugging another, but smaller body, tightly in embrace. The gasps of breathing in the room oscillated between deep sighs and lustful moaning. They slightly shifted position and, from where he stood, James saw the bewilderment and submission on Zach's face as he silently endured this nocturnal ritual. Or was it an expression of mournful ecstasy? He couldn't be sure.

James felt blood draining out of his brain and thought he would faint. He got down, picked up the stool and walked away as if in a trance. He wondered why he was so agitated, so depressed. He wiped his runny nose with his sleeve, leaned on the wall outside, hidden in shadows and looked up at the dark sky above. There were no stars.

James tried to hate Zach, cold-shouldering his advances of friendship during the ensuing days. He did not gather enough courage to face his friend and he felt betrayed. But why should he feel that way? Was he jealous of not having the forbidden fruit that he protected all these while devoured by the wild beasts beyond his control? Was he lamenting his own helplessness to prevent the breach against his friend? Was he devastated by the fall of the demigod that he held in heroic esteem in the revered glass house? What loss was he mourning? Who was he to the two of them, to feel betrayed like this?

8

Many are Called—Few Chosen

It was the first Sunday of his fourth year in the Minor Seminary and James had gone for a lone and meditative walk, when the new batch of Aspirants—brought in by the fisherman for the diocese, Father Aloysius—arrived.

Among them was one 'late vocation' that had joined after completing his under graduation and he would be directly placed with the fourth year Postulants. The term referred to those preparing for their novitiate, reportedly the most testing year of priestly formation.

James could not hold his surprise when, walking into his dormitory, he found Matthias standing tall and handsome as ever, smiling from ear to ear.

He had heard about the expected new arrival into the team from some of the seniors, but never could have guessed it would be his old friend. He went up and hugged Matthias, who responded with equal warmth. James was genuinely glad that he was there. He needed someone to lean on and there was no one he could depend on in the team, as all of them looked up to James for his leadership.

Matthias always wanted to dedicate his life to helping people and weighed all his options before choosing to follow the path of priesthood. He was also a strong believer in God and the overall goodness of people, but with a practical view to what happened around him. He hated the evil ways of the world but instead of decrying it, like most, he wanted to get really involved and change things for the best. His idealism was more grounded in reality.

Matthias did not take more than a month to become the star of, not only their batch, but of all the junior and senior seminarians. He was charismatic, genuine in his friendliness and firm in his beliefs. That, however, didn't prevent him from having a good time with his friends, pulling their legs and having a ball.

Over the years, an active indifference was built up between James and Zach, though it took some time for Zach to realise that his friend was avoiding him. Because James was the default organizer and leader for most events and activities, when he avoided someone in the team, it was tough for them to be involved in whatever was happening in the seminary. Zach found himself isolated though there was never any real confrontation between him and his former friend. James still liked Zach but he feared rebuilding that bridge. He had felt intense urge to be both emotionally and physically with Zach, to open up and confess what he had seen, and even give way to his own feelings for him. But then again, James was could not bring himself to confront much like the way he kept aloof from Elena years ago.

As he grew older, Zacharia also began to grow independent, thinking like an adult and creating his own outlook on life and people. His traumatic encounters with the man who the whole world thought of as holy, had dented his self-image and he had come to despise himself. He had blamed himself for being the victim of the older man's erotic attraction—the victim's own guilty conscience.

It took a long time, and interaction with some genuine seminarians, to affirm his own existence as a man, an independent person with a body and mind of his own.

Arrival of Matthias and his fast elevation as the leader helped Zach. The new leader found a role for everyone when any large scale events were being planned. In a few weeks of his joining he had found Zach more isolated and lacking in confidence and had decided to pull the poor guy out of his cage.

Matthias appointed him the transportation in-charge of picnic, organiser for cultural events, encouraged him to write his poetry which, with the permission of Father Philip, were displayed at the community notice board.

Zach found himself talking to people that he was too conscious of approaching, he found himself managing a group of juniors at some assignment and being applauded at the dinner table for having written an interesting poem on a butterfly.

"Zach will deliver the introduction of the topic," said Matthias as a small group of seminarians sat around. The discussion was on social awareness and involvement of the clergy, a debate to be staged in the following week.

"I will gather material for you all to speak, but I cannot deliver the talk," protested Zach meekly.

"Why can't you?" asked Matthias.

"He is afraid of the stage. Never went up there," said George, one of the seniors.

"I will write the speech if someone else can deliver it," Zach found a way out.

"Zach. You will write the speech for sure. But you will deliver it too," Matthias smiled. "If you get stuck, read it out. But I am sure, if you practice well you won't need the paper at all."

"But . . ." Zach was still reluctant and some of the others were apprehensive too.

"Zach delivering the introduction of our topic is my responsibility. I will spend some time with him every day and am fully confident of the outcome," Matthias assured them.

Everyone was taken aback the next week when Zach delivered a thoroughly prepared speech, with loud and emotional voice and almost feverish pitch. He was rebellious in his thoughts, felt passionately for the lack of social involvement among clergy and gave went to his anger. They had never seen him in such assertive voice or body language. He was vociferous enough to hide his own insecurity.

Later during the debate too, he lost his cool and confronted one of his opponents with equally loud protestations and arguments. Matthias had to pull him down to his seat and pacify him.

"What do they think? They can shout us to silence?" he was fuming.

James was absolutely at loss of words in such change of character in Zach. Looking into his eyes, he knew the guy was still insecure and self-depreciating deep within but projected an aggressive façade.

After the debate, while they gathered at the refectory for dinner, Zach thanked Matthias. Many seminarians came up to him and shook his hand. "You said what many of us did not have the guts to say," they remarked. "well written, well delivered," said others.

Matthias continue to invest his time on Zach, trying to convert this spark of confidence and aggression into a much deeper personality development. Over many days, he felt that while there was much improvement, there were some dark corners in Zach that he could not reach out to and wherein lay the foundation of his fragility. However, external changes were dramatic enough to be noticed by everyone.

As the year passed by Zach increasingly began to assert himself loudly, as if to assure himself, showing off in occasional bouts of aggression. Yet, most of the time he was the usual mild self.

He gradually created his own philosophy of the world around him with a strong leaning towards those who were repressed and marginalised by society. He felt like a victim and felt for victims of all types of exploitation in the society. He read voraciously and brooded over what he had learned; a righteous anger building up within him, that not many could see through his otherwise benevolent demeanour.

Matthias had already noticed that there was no relationship between James and Zach, despite the fact that they were in the same batch for many years, ate at the same place, studied in the same class, played together and shared the same dormitory. Since he was close to both of them, it was impossible to ignore how they avoided each other.

"The cold war is a matter of the past." Matthias read aloud from one of the newspapers when he was alone with James in the study room. The USSR was no more and the threat of another explosive world war—that had hung over them all for over three long decades—had almost vanished. James agreed.

"Unfortunately, there seems to be a cold war still going on within the team," said Matthias, looking up at his friend.

"What do you mean?"

"I mean you and Zach," he said. "It's obvious that it's going on, but no one knows why there is no more friendship between the two of you. There seems to be no reason at all. All I hear is that you were the best chums in the first two years and all of sudden things changed for the worst between you."

"I don't know why," dismissed James. "But I suppose we lost interest along the way."

"I don't believe you, Jamie. I have noticed how you behave in his presence. You are not quite yourself. There is something you are not telling me," Matthias was not buying any bullshit.

"None of your business!" James got up and walked off. Later that night he couldn't sleep. Matthias was his school friend; he had shared much with him and had valued his advice as a boy. He respected him and admired him. Yet, when he asked this morning, he was afraid to confide. Could he talk about what he had witnessed that night in Father Mark's room? Could he justify his own strange physical attraction to Zach? James had enough confidence that, with Matthias, he should not worry about discreetness in keeping the secret. What he feared was whether he would lower himself in his friend's esteem. Will he look at him as weird?

He brooded over miserably for the next two days, prayed and meditated. Then one night after the prayers when everyone sat down to study, he walked up to

Matthias in silence, left a small slip of paper in the open book in front of him.

"Meet me on the terrace"

When the two of them were alone on the terrace, munching on ground nuts and watching the stars, James spoke of his friendship with Zacharia. He couldn't really place the blame on anyone but his own feelings. Matthias listened patiently and did not show any sign of surprise or resentment. In the moonlight, James saw only understanding and acceptance. James was relieved at the end of it and felt much more at ease with himself.

"Jamie, I realise that we have grown up. Most of what is happening is natural. The way I know you, as passionate and romantic, it is nothing unusual that you feel like this. I think in some way, you had seen Elena in Zach. May be in his dependence on you, may be in his girl-like fragility or even in his physical attributes. You just transported those suppressed feelings to your new friend."

"Where is Elena now?" asked James after a long silence.

"Why are you asking me?" Matthias voice suddenly turned reproaching and James was surprised.

"Well, I thought you guys got along well in the final year. And anyway, I had decided to join seminary," said James.

"I got along well yes. But you loved her, right?" Matthias was angry now. "And what did you do? Just hide yourself from her, lock yourself at home without a word?"

"She kind of lost interest in me," James said sadly. *I left her because you, the more desirable one, could have her,* he thought.

"She lost interest? You should have been mad, Jamie, not to have seen and recognised the way that girl loved you," he looked straight at his friend. James was a bit shaken by such accusing tone of voice from Matthias. He was confused.

"The poor girl was so desolate that you were avoiding her, then completely cutting off all contacts and finally running away to become a priest. Why did you love her if you were going to be a priest?" Paused Matthias but continued without waiting for James' answer in a more amicable voice.

"Depressed, she had withdrawn from the world around her, she had none to confide. You know I was in Muscat and had no clues about your decision to leave. I should have noticed when you were drifting away, but I don't know how I missed it," he said.

"When her parents proposed to send her to a boarding school in Ooty, she agreed, in an attempt to leave the memories of her lost love. At least, you should have explained why you were dumping her unceremoniously," he stopped.

James felt an ache somewhere. His eyes became misty.

"When she came for vacation after three months I met her. She had not still gotten over with you. She told me that not a day passed without thinking of you. What did the poor girl do to you that you gift her such pain?" He asked. James could not control himself any longer.

"It's my fault. I doubted her love. I thought she liked you," he was almost in tears.

"What? Me?" Matthias looked shocked and amused at the same time. There was a long silence.

"At least shouldn't you have asked? Was I not your friend? Couldn't you ask her?" he was now able to join the scattered pieces to get a clear picture.

"I felt, if she wanted so, you were better match for her," James said.

"You are a bigger nut than I thought," Matthias now lay on the floor and James sat next to him.

"I mentored and nurtured her talents but your views were blinded by your romance that you ignored that I did that for many people, not just Elena," Matthias was now finding the whole thing a comedy or errors—but what a tragic experience for the two love birds of his school.

"I think that was it. I was so possessive and imagined many things. I can never forgive myself for what I did to her," James sat looking away.

"It is now almost five years and things have all changed. She must have got along well somewhere. I lost touch long ago. Yet, to think of her as in love with me—you have been a fool," Matthias tried to laugh.

James too lay on his back and looked up at the sky. What a fool he had been! Then they both burst out into laughter and kicked the air with both their legs.

Some years later, the two of them would dismiss Elena's case as Jamie's tryst with puppy love, which could never qualify as true love. Love was a mature, responsible emotion and not the throbbing of two young desperate hearts. For them, as the chosen of God, love was not directed only at one person but at the whole world, to wish well for all and act for the wellbeing of everyone.

James had made peace with himself after that long night of confession with Matthias. He had to get it over with Zach now.

The following Sunday, James, for the first time in four years, smiled at Zach when they met on the way to the refectory for lunch. Zach was a bit surprised but smiled back at James.

"Shall we go for a walk this evening, you and me alone?" asked James.

"Sure," Zach agreed.

"You were my closest friend in the first year," James said not fully knowing where to start. Zach nodded as the two strolled alone that evening.

"I still remember those days when we used to go for walks, sit together, eat together. The first picnic and our return journey," James said. Zach smiled and walked alongside.

"Then one day, I just stopped talking to you," said James and looked at Zach.

"Yes, why did you?" he asked. James thought silently for some time not sure how to open up.

"I think I saw something I felt, kind of uneasy about, something not so right," he said. Zach tensed up but continued walking. He buried his hands deep in his pants' pockets.

"I saw you one night in Father Mark's room, midnight," James said looking away, finding it difficult to face Zach.

Zach grew pale and stopped walking. There was a long pause and both of them did not speak for a long time. Then they resumed walking.

"I was too naïve then, or I was confused that I had similar feelings for you," James said slowly. Zach did not respond. "I didn't know how to confront you. I was kind of angry and depressed. May be it's my fault that I was somewhat possessive of you, I think," James confessed.

"I tried to detach myself from you, more because I feared myself. I never hated you," James now looked at Zach.

"It happened. I was too scared and did not know how to resist him," said Zach, his eyes looking no were. "He used me, betrayed my trust in him. It happened two or three times before I started avoiding him or going to him alone."

James listened.

"I lost your friendship too. You were the only close friend I had and I just withdrew further into a shell," he said wearily. "I hate that man all the more for it now."

"I am sorry, Zach. I won't hurt you again," said James. And they hugged each other. There were tears in their eyes and did now know how long they stood that way. Once again, after a gap of years, they walked around hand in hand and talked of things that they had not shared for a long time—feeling lighter for laying down the load they carried for so long.

Matthias was the first to notice and rejoice at the change in Zach and James and renewal of their friendship. James thanked him for opening his eyes.

James and Zach were no longer the timid and the protector, and there was no more cuddling and hugging but they could talk, work and live together. Zach knew what pleased James and did not hold anything back from his naturally dominant friend. Yet, he was now a person with his own body and will, not a victim anymore.

Zach felt liberated deep inside when he got his friend back again. It had given him an opportunity, for the first time, to talk about the abuse he had undergone and his own guilt feeling as a victim. The stronger he became inside, the more visible was his self confidence that it bequeathed respect from others. With some help from Matthias, he asserted his own personality—his identity as Zacharia Tharakan. He was no more a powerless victim but a person with power over himself. He would extend that to the rest of the world someday—he promised himself silently and sternly.

Postulancy was over and they were more than three months into their Noviciate. There were more prayers, more work and more days of fasting and abstinence in Noviciate.

Unaffected by all these changes, Johny-the-horny continued to be the chief organiser of all unofficial mid-night get-togethers. He did his role with exceptional discretion, perfectly coordinating with all parties involved. His reputation had grown so much that even some of the seniors and priests took part in exclusive drinking sessions and porno screenings. True to the bible phrase, 'the left hand shall not know what the right hand is doing', he compartmentalised his clientele and sessions to save embarrassment to any. He even managed to save some money from all these transactions, using it to cover his own expenses and to pay for trips home during summer vacations.

It was at the end of fifth year that Johny told his two old friends about his plan to leave the pursuit of priesthood and enter the real world. Owing to many years of alcohol abuse, his father had developed cirrhosis of the liver and stomach ulcers that threatened to turn malignant. He was now bed-ridden unable to even hold a glass of the brandy he so desperately wanted. Johny's mother was struggling to feed the family, buy medicine for her ailing husband and take care of three daughters.

During her long and tearful telephone calls with Johny, she would list out her misery in the ascending order, sighing in the beginning, weeping midway and finishing with a prolonged wail. Johny hated these sessions but now he realised that he could no longer run away from reality.

If only he could get out, take up some job and support his family, he could have some peace.

He needed to make money, and a lot of it, to cover all daily expenses and save up enough to get his three sisters married. He could continue living in the safety within the four walls of the seminary and turn his senses away from real life, in the name of serving the Lord, but he found that idea extremely disturbing.

After sharing this with his friends, Johny met Father Timothy, who was their Master that year, and informed him about his decision. Unlike Philip Kurien, Father Timothy was understanding and appreciated Johny's courage to plunge into life, though he was not happy to let anyone leave the path of priesthood.

So on a weary afternoon in April, Johny said goodbye to his friends, batch mates and many grieving clients and walked away with his old backpack into the real world of working and earning one's living.

By the time they reached the year of philosophical studies, the batch had shrunk to just twelve. Some had left on their own and others had been sent off for various reasons, including pilfering funds, sleeping consistently through prayer sessions, failing in qualifying examinations, hitting a senior priest publically and even for groping a nun.

The philosophy program included community outreach programs. As philosophy students, the seminarians had to work with local communities. It required them to organise food and shelter for the poor, help the destitute, attend to the abandoned and sick. They were being exposed to poverty that India had in abundance. Some had to live with the villagers to understand their life and propose programs to better their lives.

Some of them engaged in empowerment programs like education and self-help groups; and helping to build houses for the homeless. This work, combined with the various courses they had on social and political philosophy, exposed them to the complex reality of the exploitation of the poor, the significance and origin of the Communist and other resistance movements, the revolutionary praxis of modern day liberation theologians and the socialist movements within the church in different parts of the world.

In most parts of the world, Christianity was viewed as a powerful tool wielded by the capitalists and the conquerors. However, there were also priests who closely empathised with the sufferings of the poor and the marginalised and advocated on their behalf in South America, Africa and some parts of India. There were also many armchair theologians who wrote volumes on Jesus' option for the poor and churned out eloquent books on the so called 'liberation theology'. Yet the fact remained that while six million children died of hunger across the continents every year, no priest ever did.

James and Zach were also sent to such programs and in the process learned that the weak were always confined to the side-lines. Most of the workers had no right to their produce, most farmers did not own land, and many workers were only given food and no wages. Money and power collided in a few hands that ensured the poor stayed in poverty eternally.

They were assigned to a remote village in Andhra Pradesh to increase the literacy level of the tribal folks and other farm workers. The village was practically created by an influential landlord who had illegally converted large extend of forest land into cultivation, displacing many tribals and forcing them to work in his farm just for food.

During their two months' stay there, James and Zach were once pulled up by their superiors for leading the local farmers in a strike against Landlord. They were overwhelmed by the malnutrition of the kids, the raping and tormenting of women and mistreatment of workers. They had encouraged the women to read, write and obtain alternate sources of income, found ways for the kids to go to school, helped the schools to provide mid-day meals, and assisted the men in demanding better wages. The landlord had warned them of serious consequences but the two young seminarians had gone ahead and organised a rally to the local MLA's house demanding an end to the exploitation.

There were some calls made from Landlord to the local MLA, from MLA to a Minister and a Minister spoke to the Bishop. Soon, the duo was packed off unceremoniously. On the train back to Kunnamkulam, they spoke little to each other.

They joined back at the seminary, rebelling internally and mentally committing themselves to the emancipation of the downtrodden—each in his own way.

James was the more upset of the two. Even Matthias could not pacify him.

"Eight years, Matthias," James asked "what have I been doing here?"

"I agree my coming here was accidental but I found a meaning later-on. I wanted to be a priest so that I can serve the people. But here I am, joining hands with those who exploit them!" he told Matthias who asked him to pray over it for some time.

For more than a year James had been disturbed by the dichotomy of beliefs and practice. He was a faithful member of the Church and was being prepared for priesthood, so he had a responsibility to the sustenance and growth of the official machinery. At the same time he realised with each passing day that the servants of his Church were more concerned in protecting the administrative structure than in practicing the way of the Lord.

Jesus was not a conformist, he exhibited a clear preference for the poor and the sinners, and he did not have any worldly position of authority; instead used the influence of his own divine personality.

Yet, his so called followers and the proclaimed guardians of his teachings—the Church—were just the opposite. Its representatives lacked conviction; they were obsessed with elaborate structure of their organisation, lording over believers. They imposed chastity, poverty and obedience on themselves—whether Jesus wanted it or not—and secretly lamented what they missed. They played second fiddle to the rich and mighty, in effect, securing their own safety and comfort. They preached and prayed in comfort, never having to worry about the next meal on their table, while the real people of God starved.

James had stayed in the seminary, leaving behind a bright future in academia and as a sportsman, his wealthy inheritance and the girl he loved—only to dedicate himself to the service of the Lord. He realised that he wasn't doing anything at all for the good of His people. He was in shackles manufactured by the officialdom of his institutionalized religion. He felt that his actions, dictated by the prescriptions of his superiors, were not in line with what he believed in and with what Jesus expected his followers to do.

He finally decided to quit, running away from the cognitive dissonance that haunted him.

9

A Second Life

His mother was disappointed that her son would not don the holy cassock and offer the Holy Mass at the altar. A priest in the family was a prestige for everyone, often with the exception of the guy himself.

His father was glad that his son has come back and would carry own the family's name down the generations when he got married and had children of his own. He was also glad that his son was not doing something that he did not enjoy or believe in doing.

On his return, James tried to find out where Johny was. He was told that his old friend had wandered around for a couple of months in hopes of finding a job. Agitated by the futility of his efforts and the condition of his family, he had taken an overnight train to Madras. It seems he found some job there with a small firm, earned enough to keep himself alive and send home occasional money orders.

After a year, Johny had started some business of his own and thrived enough to send home generous amount of money, get a home nurse to attend to his ailing father, buy expensive clothes and gold for his mother and sisters. In two years, he had bought a reasonably good house and the family moved there. James even heard that Johny had bought a huge cardamom estate near Munnar. One of his sisters was married off to a bank clerk, lived in Kottayam and was reportedly happy.

It took James some asking around to find where Johny's family now lived. They were still within the same parish but closer to the town than they were in their miserable days.

"He comes home only once a year. Madras is just an overnight journey," his mother complained when James had gone to see her. Johny's father was moving around within the house but was mostly confined to the four walls. Despite all that Johny was doing, he kept cursing everyone around for not letting him handle money or go to the town for his drinks. His constitution was still in tatters and James felt his life would leave him if he had as much as a good sneeze—let alone alcohol.

Arrival of wealth had not brought peace to this family. May be that is the reason for Johny's reluctance in visiting it often. He did his responsibility to the family by providing for them, but James felt that his friend did not love them enough to be with them.

James called on the mobile number Johny's mother had given him.

"Oh my!" Johny gave a cry of excitement when he heard his friend's voice, "That's like a man! Congrats for leaving the fucking seminary," he sounded delighted.

He said there is a great world abundant with opportunities for the discerning.

"What magic you do in Madras to make so much money?" asked James.

"That is a long story, someday I will write an autobiography," he laughed aloud amused at his own joke. "In simple words, I am a real estate agent."

"Is there so much money in real estate?" asked James.

"There is money in all business provided you know how to strike at the right time and the right way," Johny beamed.

"You seem to have struck gold," James agreed.

"Well, if you can forget all that you learned in school and seminary, then you can also be successful in this," he said.

"I will find my own way. I am keen to try civil services," said James.

"Cool. You live by the rules; I thrive by breaking them. All the best!" Johny liked this comparison. He extended his invitation to visit Madras.

"In a few months from now I will not be in Madras, but Chennai. They are changing the name of this city. That won't change my fortune!" he signed off in style.

Even before James had packed off from Seminary in late August, he had a plan for his future. He spent the next six months preparing for the civil service examinations. He had the advantage of reading newspapers and periodicals regularly and having his own view on most current affairs.

He did well in his UPSC prelims, cracked the main and personality rounds comfortably and joined the Indian Police Service (IPS) as a part of the Tamil Nadu cadre.

He was outstanding during his training years and soon earned a reputation for his intelligence, physical strength and endurance.

Once during the training the team was sent for a mock hunt for a criminal in hiding to a village in Madhya Pradesh. They were told that they had to capture Chandu Bali a notorious criminal who had now taken shelter in a vast wasteland near Sirsi.

Shabib Hassan, a smart trainee from the batch was chosen to lead the team. James was given the responsibility to recce the place before the team landed. Kattar Singh was assigned as his companion in this task. They had to observe the location, identify possible hiding locations of Chandu, identify the most effective route to get there and launch an attack—all this without being noticed by anyone.

They had to crawl at many places, had lost their way couple of times, ran out of food and water in nearly 36 hours of expedition. Kattar was almost down by the end of the day but James egged him on.

"Man, I cannot move any longer. Let's rest for five minutes," Kattar sat down leaning against a tree.

"We have very less time and any lack of alertness will mean our man might escape from this area itself," said James.

"I can't," he sat there.

"Then do one thing, sit this side, no one will see you here. I will get you when I come back," James was off leaving Kattar wondering.

Kattar had a good sleep by the time James returned after several hours.

"There is no more to do at this place," he said and Kattar followed him.

"So what is the picture like?" asked Kattar.

"I will explain when we get back to the base. Let us get out of here quickly," he pulled his companion by the sleeve and Kattar could only obey.

Back in the tent, James drew a map on a large sheet of paper and explained the possible hideouts and ways of attack. He was sure where the criminal is based on some signs of habitation he had observed, including *beedi* stubs, dry chicken bones and egg shells.

To everyone's surprise, James did not stop at explaining the result of his recce but went on to outlining the entire operation plan. Shabib was not amused.

"Excuse me, James" he said. "I suppose I lead this mission?"

"Oh, yes. Then as the leader of our team you should do this . . ." and continued to tell him how the operation should be conducted.

Though he wanted to protest, Shabib soon felt that James was not trying to steal the limelight from him but genuinely believed that his plan was the best. And others seem to think the same as well and at some point Shabib too agreed that this was the best strategy.

Kattar was shocked when James said they commence to operation the same day.

"I want to have some *aloo paratha* and chicken curry. And yes, one glass of *Lassi*," he shouted. Everyone broke into laughter but that did not deter Kattar.

"Are you some machine? No sleep and no food for two days. Still saying let's go right away?" he asked James.

Saravanan who was responsible for logistics had arranged for enough food for all and they ate before starting off the operation.

The team realised that the whole exercise was a set up by their trainers only after securing a dummy criminal—a goat tied to a pole in a cave. They were congratulated for following the right process, gathering useful intelligence surreptitiously. Kattar was sad that he missed his meals to chase an imaginary criminal.

James could work continuously at something with sustained concentration, skipping sleep and food when required. This was not limited to physical action but extended to detailed research and report writing.

As Assistant Commissioner of Police, Law and Order, in Coimbatore, James' first two years were a test of his abilities and character.

In less than a week of his taking charge, a dark fat guy in pure whites walked in to his office. The constable on duty introduced him as Paramasivam, owner of a textile processing unit in town.

"Sir, good morning," he sat down as soon as he came.

"Good Morning. Mr Paramasivam?"

"Yes, you know me already, sir. Then half my job is done," he smiled from ear to ear.

"What is the purpose of this visit? Any complaints?" asked James

"No. no. sir. Just wanted to say hello to the new ACP, that's all," he smiled.

"Thanks," James indicated that it was time to wind up pleasantries. Paramasivam got up.

"Sir, I will meet you at your residence," and walked off without waiting for a response.

He called Sub Inspector Vijay Kumar.

"I thought he would come," was his response. "He is an absolute crook. There is a criminal investigation going on against him. Man slaughter. One of his troublesome workers found dead under suspicious circumstances."

"Let me study the case. The file is—let me see—right here," said James.

Paramasivam and many others were in for a shock when the new ACP threw them out along with their gifts from his residence. His predecessor had been benevolent to such benefactors and this change was unwelcome to many in the city.

In his spare time, James would roam around in a cheap set of *veshti* and shirt in a friend's Yamaha Rx100, visiting the lanes of the city unnoticed.

With some help from Johny, he was able to befriend some of the 'boys' of the street. They did all kinds of odd jobs for a living, legal or illegal—most of the time latter. They worked as good source for further contacts and information when needed. James was not interested in the small fish but the sharks that had infested the city.

In all the cases he worked on he had a knack of cracking the hardest of criminals and tracing the route of the problem. In most cases, as the trail lead upwards from organised crime to political godfathers, senior officers took over the case and James developed a detachment about whatever became of the investigation.

He, however, he kept track of them for academic reasons.

Though there were moments of despair, when credit for some investigation that he had skilfully carried out was bestowed on someone else, he never sulked over it. In India, there was no scarcity of crimes; only the lack of smart police officers who could deal with them.

He had taken a day off that Sunday to do some shopping and to attend the wedding of one of his staff members. Tired after shuttling around the whole day, he called up Satish, a local confidant who worked as a bearer in one of the city hotels. Satish was introduced to him by Johny and was well connected with city's various gangs who were involved in pretty crimes and theft.

By the time Satish arrived in his bike, James was ready in his *veshti* and shirt. They roamed around the city for a while and then settled down at a crowded local wine shop. James ordered Old Monk, a coke and bottle of water while Satish settled for a bottle of Haywards beer.

"Have you met quarter Kesavan?" Satish asked.

"No. Doesn't ring a bell," said James.

"The one there on far right, sitting along with the fat bald guy," indicated Satish. James saw a lean and hungry looking guy with high cheek bones and sharp pointy hair.

"He is part of the gang that pedal in counterfeit liquor. You name the bottle and he has a counterfeit," said Satish. "Did you notice? Quarter has been looking at us for some time now. I think he has something to tell me," said Satish.

"Go ahead," said James and lighted his cigarette.

Satish was right. The moment he got up and stepped out, the pointy haired guy followed leaving his companion to drink alone.

Satish returned only after twenty minutes. Quarter Kesavan was not with him.

"Let us go to another place," he told James. Without asking any questions, James got up, pulled out two hundred notes from his pocket and handed over the waiter as he walked out.

Hopping on to Satish's bike the two of them went to a small roof top bar just half a kilometre away. They found quarter Kesavan sitting in one corner and joined him.

After placing their orders with a boy who acted as waiter, James looked quizzically at Satish.

"Quarter here tells me that there are some new boys in town," said Satish. Quarter was looking curiously at James.

"Oh, this is my friend James. He works in the security team in our hotel," Satish introduced.

"Oh, good," Kesavan seemed satisfied with the answer. A friend of Satish could be trusted.

"What's special about the new boys?" asked James.

"Sir, it is kind of strange. They don't look like us. Initially we thought they were from Kerala because they spoke Tamil with some difficulty and looked fairer like the Muslim boys from Malappuram," said Kesavan.

"May be they are," said James.

"No. When alone, they speak only Hindi. And they are taller than the Kerala boys. Secondly, they do not seem to work anywhere and spend their time mostly in the room or roaming around in twos and threes," Kesavan emptied his glass of brandy in one gulp and licked on a piece of pickled lime.

"Aren't there guys coming for all over the country, looking for some job?"

"They should be looking for job, right? Not scouting for old scooters?" said Kesavan. "There is a place outside the city where some of our guys run a dismantling unit for stolen vehicles. Two of the boys were there trying to buy one of those."

"That is a point," said Satish.

"Someone tells me they were well loaded with money," said Kesavan.

"Do you know where they live?" asked James.

"I found out this morning," Kesavan had finished his second glass now.

They ordered a plate of scrambled eggs more to get the waiter boy away.

Kesavan explained that there were some six of them altogether but never seen together except in the room. A boy who supplied milk in the area had seen them in a first floor room which was rented out by a local tea-shop vendor himself occupying the ground floor.

"I think they are here for some mischief. Must be some jewellery or bank robbery," said Satish. "I have heard of such gangs travelling from city to city across the country."

Satish told Kesavan to be discreet about this information so that the boys are not alerted by unnecessary attention. He said James in his security job knew people who could find information and help.

James suggested that Kesavan keeps low and inform Satish as soon as he gets any new piece of information.

When they were alone riding back home James felt he needed to explore this a bit. He knew the area well and decided to spend the night there.

With some help from quarter Kesavan, James located the house. There were couple of windows to the room housing the boys. The only building nearby that could possibly offer a view was blocked by a huge mango tree. James had to wait till it was very late for the place to be completely deserted.

Then he climbed on to the tree and used his powerful binoculars to have a good look at the place. He could see five guys at different points in time. Most of the time they were at a corner that he could not see but he watched them crisscrossing the room several times. Then a sixth guy passed the window for the first time. He had a soldering gun in his hand. James' senses were alerted.

He slowly moved to a different branch feeling his way in darkness. There were two guys sitting on the floor with a laptop. The screen was facing against James and he hoped they would turn around some time at least for a brief moment.

Then he saw it, reflecting on the spectacles of one of the guys in front of the laptop—google map enlarging and contracting. It was too unclear to know details. In an hour or so, the light was off and the guys had gone to sleep.

James slowly climbed down, walked quietly for a kilometre. There were a few night taxis at the nearby hospital and he hailed one of them to go back to his residence.

The next night with a handful of policemen in mufti, James, shadowed each of the guys when they stepped out, unceremoniously bundled them into their vehicles at unsuspecting places. Two were picked up from the room along with incriminating evidence of a plan to explode a powerful bomb. The bomb was ready and they had managed to fix a timer. There were couple of pistols and a few rounds of ammunition.

"They were planning to blow up the union Home Minister," said James sitting across the commissioner's office later that day. Home Minster was to visit Coimbatore in two days' time for the inauguration of an international conference on 'changing times and challenges in law or order' at the Codissia Complex.

"The boys have begun to sing already but we need to trace back the conspirators," James said.

"This is audacious!"

"They came down all the way from Kashmir to take him out at Coimbatore," said James.

"This was not a high profile meeting and hence they would know that the security would be just normal," said the commissioner.

"Sir, I am going after them," James got up.

"James," Commissioner followed him to the door. "You did a great job today. You saved our jobs. If the old man had been blasted off, we would all be nowhere," he sighed.

James did not respond. Saving the commissioner's job was not his concern but saving the life of a minister, or any law abiding citizen was.

James made some quick progress in his investigation when he was informed about his promotional transfer to Chennai city.

The news of the attempt to murder the Home Minister had reached the senior most levels in the state and union governments and James was appreciated for his timely action. Media too picked up the story and kind of made a hero out of the ACP.

This finally resulted in his being called to Chennai, the centre of all action.

In Chennai too, the number of James' well-wishers was soon outnumbered by the enemies he earned from the illegal cartels and corrupt leaders. However, there were a few—in the department and in government—who believed in him and backed him up in his clean-up efforts.

During his stay and earlier visits to Chennai he met Johny and was really surprised to see the changes that the once famished boy had gone through. He lived in the upmarket Alwarpet area in a well-furnished three bedroom flat, juggled three expensive mobile phones, drank imported liquor, wore branded shirts and jeans and owned a Honda CRV.

He had acquired much wealth in meddling with real estate deals. One of his modus operandi was to obtain the power of attorney from the owner after having negotiated a competitive price for the property. He would then pay an advance promising to register the property later. He would delay—in some pretext or other—till the prices move upward. When he found the price good enough and had a buyer the registration is carried out. The original seller would meet the actual buyer only at the registration office. He would never know the selling price.

He also took large portions of agricultural land, converted into plots and sold for huge profits. Approvals were available for an extra fee. As he became powerful he had the wherewithal to force the vulnerable to sell at the price he quoted. If he had his eyes on a property, he would send his goons to create enough trouble for the reluctant owner until he agrees to sell the property. Local police were tipped to keep a tight lip.

James did not dive deep into Johny's affairs but his friend's contacts in Chennai were useful to him.

He had spent another two years in Chennai when he had a direct call from the DGP's office. Mr. Arunachalam was one of the senior most officers in Tamilnadu police, one of the few who held important positions during alternating governments. He was a man of practical wisdom and knew a good talent when he found one.

James stood respectfully in the large chamber.

"Sit down, James," he said to the younger officer and he obeyed.

"I have heard good things about you," said Arunachalam.

"Sir," admitted James.

Then there was a shuffle of feet at the door.

"Welcome, Mr Subramanian!" said the DGP looking over his shoulders.

James turned around to see the home secretary walking in. He quickly seated himself next to James. Subramanian was a tall, lean man with sharp features. He was soft spoken but that was just opposite of what he really was—a determined, ruthless, decisive and task oriented bureaucrat. Most of the senior police officers feared him as much as they hated him. Interestingly he got along well with Arunachalam.

"Now, to get to business," he started, facing James. "We are taking you out from your current assignment."

"Sir?" James did not know whether it was a snub.

"There is something more important that we want you to work on. Something that needs a clinical brain and a matching hand," he said. James was now all attention.

"You might have already heard how our force has been fighting the Naxal menace along the Western Ghats," said DGP.

"Yes. I know it has not yielded the results we were looking for," said James.

"Precisely. Their style of operation and support of the local residents are making it difficult for us to progress. They have killed many of our men in ambush and landmine blasts," continued Arunachalam.

"We have intelligence inputs that they have sophisticated weapons, smuggled from China and other countries. They reach the Satyamangalam forests through various channels—mostly via Nepal and Bengal. Naxals of Jharkand, Orissa and Andhra Pradesh are all linked through a powerful network," explained Subramanian.

"Sir, I understand the locals are a big support for them. The naxals have effectively positioned themselves as their saviours. We are also to be blamed that our developmental schemes have not reached these poor people and exploitation by the rich have been going on for decades. They are easily influenced when they find a resistance that promise them better lives," said James. He was not sure whether he had spoken out of line.

"Frankly, I should agree," said Subramanian. "This is our own creation."

"Like Frankenstein's monster!" said the DGP. "The sad truth is, under this cover they smuggle sandal wood and ivory, buy sophisticated weapons in the international black markets and kill our own people."

"The Chief Minister has consented to form a discreet Special Task Force (STF) to clean this up," said Subramanian.

"You will lead this team," Arunachalam looked at James to see his reaction. James sat silent.

"When we say team, we are not talking about a large contingent of policemen. We mean ten to fifteen officers who can track the leaders down and arrest them," said Subramanian.

"The state police will continue their routine resistance. The formation of STF will be known to only a handful of us. The risk is great for the government and for you," continued the Home secretary. "Especially to the chief minister because he has not consulted his party or council of ministers and is taking this up at his personal risk. He is afraid that the news would leak out if more people know about it. It was not an easy decision to make but a necessary one."

"You and your team would be risking your own lives," said the DGP. "We do not have a clear estimate of their intelligence network, man or fire power."

"I understand," said James. "I need to study this."

"There is one Sub Inspector Joe who has survived a landmine blast that killed most of the policemen of a contingent that had gone to Sathyamangalam earlier this year. You can meet him after this," said Arunachalam.

Subramanian then got up and picked up his files. James stood up in attention.

"James, the Chief Minister will meet you day after tomorrow. I will inform where and when. By then you should have a team and possibly enough knowledge about the case," said the home secretary before leaving the room.

"James, let me know what you need. Name the guys you want in your team and the weapons you need. We won't spare anything!" said Arunachalam.

"Where can I find this man Joe?" asked James.

Arunachalam dialled a number and asked Joe to be sent in. In another two minutes a smart young man walked in. He saluted his seniors and stood in attention.

"Joe, this is James. From today, you will be reporting to him on a new assignment. Now, go ahead and show him what you have on the Naxal's case," ordered the DGP amiably. "Now, gentlemen, you may take your leave."

The two officers saluted and left.

James soon realised that Joe was an intelligent officer with a flair for computers and internet. He had spent some time in the cyber investigation team before moving to field operations. James had already formed his team in his mind. Leo the sharpshooter, Avira the black-belt and Joe along with six others would form his team.

In two days he had a meeting with the Chief Minister—brief and clear. He wanted result in the shortest possible time and it had to be in his administration's favour.

The STF had orders to engage and capture the naxalites leaders, Thirunavukarasu, aka Thiru and Subashchandrabose, alias Bose, and their five member forest cabinet. Unofficially, the Chief Minister had given them the licence to empty their AK-47s on every naxalite standing against them, man or woman.

It took two weeks of intelligence gathering, mostly incognito, by James and his core team, before they were ready to enter the forests. In the process they managed to convince some of the villagers to turn informers with a promise to help them out of their oppressive masters—the local landlords.

Before the team left for Sathyamangalam forests, James had presented a list of actions that the government will have to do to rehabilitate the poor people of the nearby villages if any action against the naxals had to yield lasting solution.

"We can capture some of them today, but if this social condition continues, a thousand will rise again," he said to the Home Secretary. The poverty and misery he had witnessed there had emboldened him to speak thus to one of the most powerful people in the State.

"I will do the needful," assured Subramanian. "Wish you all the best!"

Three days later, five of the leaders were captured alive, more than twenty naxals were killed and James had lost five of his nine men.

While the media and politicians celebrated the success, James sat downcast along with his three subordinates, Joe, Leo and Avira mourning their valiant teammates.

Leo was the most enraged as most of them had been his team members for a long time, even before he had joined James. He wanted to shoot the captured naxal leaders in retaliation but James had to force him out of it. No one would have known if the five were finished off in the forest and that would have served them better than the long drawn judicial process of the state, he had argued.

It was after a week when the team met up with the DGP and Home Secretary. After the initial words of appreciation, James brought the discussion back to the plan he had submitted for the relief of the villagers in the affected area.

"James, I have passed on your recommendation to ministry of social welfare. They will follow this through," said Subramanian.

It took another couple of months and follow-up with different ministries—social welfare, Forests and tribal welfare—before James realised that the papers had disappeared into one of those chasm of inaction so typical of government departments.

At some point, one of the undersecretaries told him to get lost and mind his own business of policing and leave the developmental agenda to social welfare department.

He had then confronted Subramanian who expressed his helplessness. He had stormed out in agitation from the Home Secretary's office. That evening, his superiors informed James that his access to the senior bureaucrat's office should not be taken for granted.

The next day, James sent in his papers for indefinite leave. It was accepted.

10

The Pursuit begins

A middle aged man in lungi and shirt came in with two cups of coffee and some biscuits as James drummed the thick mahogany panel of the Archbishop's office table. Matthias stood near the window staring blankly at the sprawling manicured lawn outside.

It was now more than five years since James and team had captured the notorious naxal leaders from Satyamangalam forests. As Leo had warned, the court case went on endlessly and the criminals were enjoying their high profile status in the Chennai Central Prison.

"The forest here is not very familiar to me or my team. In Satyamangalam, we spent fifteen days in mufti and had invested enough time to find out more about the people, movements of the naxals, the climate and the forest routes. And there was a huge official force at our service." James leaned back on his chair.

"Here you are going to be on your own. You are neither the government nor the police. And there is no time to spare," Matthias said without turning back. "We have the funding to meet any requirements of your team. Money is no problem at all."

"I'm aware the Vatican is not poor," said James "but I think money won't help us much. Again, I don't think my focus will be to save the two Italians as much as to secure Zach's release."

Then, with an unprecedented look of determination on his face, James sprang to his feet and shook hands with Matthias, "I am on the job. You will soon hear from me. I may call from different numbers so you should pick up all incoming calls. I will make arrangements for the team and weapons. I don't want you to be entangled in controversies. After all you are the Archbishop"

And then he walked out. The driver standing near the car opened the back door and James slipped in.

"To the Airport," he said firmly when the driver was behind the steering wheel.

As the Benz fled through the highway, James called Johny on his mobile. "I will meet you at your Chennai apartment at six. I need ten SIM cards registered with addresses all across the country. I want you to find out any information you can get on the naxalite camp in the Nilambur area and nearby forests," he said without listening to the exclamations on the other end.

"James! What are you up to?" Johny was confused for a moment.

"I will speak to you in person," Johny heard the resounding seriousness in James' voice and decided not to enquire further. He had less than four hours to get his act together. He pushed off the lithesome eighteen-something Punjabi girl off his groin and began to put on his clothes. As he stormed out he threw a bunch of notes on the bed and the girl, who till then was in shock, looked at it and smiled in satisfaction—wages and bonus for an incomplete job.

The next call James made was to Joe's cell phone at the farmhouse, but only after stepping out of the car on reaching the Airport and making sure there was no one near him. Joe was at his computer when the phone began to vibrate. He updated James regarding what he had found about the Archbishop.

"We have a problem," said James, cutting him off. "Listen, there has been a kidnapping this morning. Two Vatican diplomats and a priest have been taken prisoners by Naxalites very near our own area. The priest in question is a very close friend of mine, Zacharia Tharakan. I am on the mission already."

"Back to uniform?"

"No. It is totally unofficial"

"Can we join you?"

"It's your choice. Discuss it with the guys. It may help to know that the naxalites have demanded the release of those five brigands we put behind bars five years ago." James said pausing at every word.

"Bastards!" Joe grunted.

"I am off to Chennai now and will return in a late night flight. I need to gather some information from a friend and some SIM cards," then in almost a whisper "Pick up the stuff from the underground cellar and clean it up. We'll need it"

"I'll do some research on the forests and routes through a couple of discreet connections I have. That is after I have enlisted erstwhile Constable Avira and Circle Inspector Leo." Said the once Sub Inspector of Police before hanging up.

In a few minutes the three ex-Policemen were huddled together in the dining room. They had heard about Zach, though not everything about the relationship between their boss and his seminary friend, but enough to know that James would risk anything to save his friend. Their boss had, in the past, risked his own life many times to save them and they had stuck to him like pins to a magnet.

When James had proceeded on long leave after his fallout with the Home secretary and his own superiors over their disregard for settling the displaced poor and informants of Sathyamangalam, these men had also followed him. James had moved into the large block of land in Malabar, owned by his father, they had come over one by one, initially for a few short stays and then ended up staying permanently. Joe and Leo were bachelors and in the busy uniformed life had not thought of settling down. Avira was a widower, his kids stayed in a hostel in Trichur near the Engineering College they attended.

There were three reasons why they had no second thoughts about joining this unofficial mission: First, they did not want the five men they had captured to escape their sentence; second, they were men of action—recharged by every danger they faced; finally and most importantly, James was already in it and they would not let him do it alone.

Once they were sure that none of the farm hands were in the vicinity, a secret trapdoor was opened to an inconspicuous underground cellar. Leo slipped himself in with a pen torch between his teeth while the others knelt by the side of the entrance. Then, from the depth of the little dark room, emerged Anton Kafalnikov 47s, Baretta 92s, Glock 17s and Heckler and Koch MK23s followed by a huge array of ammunitions, Leupold binoculars and their prized possession of two F-2000 Assault rifles. Leo then pulled himself up dragging a bundle of backpacks along with him. For a moment the floor looked like a war zone.

The assortments were moved quickly to one of the inner rooms and the trio got into the meticulous process of cleaning and lubricating their collection. These had all come from different parts of the world, illegally smuggled in to the country. They had captured, stolen and bought them at various occasions to build a formidable arsenal for themselves—and they were masters at using them when needed. Now, after a blissful break of five years, the time had come to use them again and they wondered whether they lacked practice.

After picking up the ticket and going through security check, James sat waiting for the boarding call, still trying to logically place the events of the day in order. From the pleasant slumber and peaceful life of the farm, he was now in the threshold of a dangerous mission. It wasn't his job anymore but for his friend he would do anything. He thought of Zach and a wave of melancholy swept through him. Some boys never grow up; he mumbled and closed his eyes. In the dimness that enveloped he saw Zach's face, as on that day in the night bus down the hair pin bends of Wynad hills. Then there was fog and chillness followed by the warmth of a shared woollen shawl.

11

Johny the Magician

It was five thirty in the afternoon when the prepaid taxi reached the upmarket apartment complex in Raja Annamalai Puram. James had called his friend from the Kamaraj Airport to make sure Johny would be at home when he arrived. After tipping the driver a fifty rupee note, he took a lift to the fifth floor and pressed the calling bell in front of door number 420. After waiting for a few seconds Johny let himself in, opening the door loudly and greeting his friend, shaking his head in disbelief. They were meeting for the first time in six years even though they had kept contact over phone.

James tapped his friend's bulging belly.

"You know, the only exercise I used to do was in bed. These days the girls don't even let me do any of the work. They just want to be on top. I am spoilt," he laughed and led his friend to the dining table.

James had not been to this apartment before and he noted that there was abundant displays of the prosperity

104

of his friend apart from his bulging tummy, including expensive paintings, a teakwood bar with an array of expensive liquors from all over the world, imported furniture and carpet, the latest LED TV with top of the class home theatre system. His friend was adorned in riches.

Over a peg of Johny Walker Blue label with a melting ice cube floating and Goldflake kings for company, James told the developments of the day in a nutshell.

"So you are going after them?"

"No. I am going after him and, in that pursuit, if I have to take them on, I will."

"You guys were pretty thick, I know. He was a nice chap; unfortunately, he ended up becoming a priest," Johny shook his head as if becoming a priest was the worst thing that could happen to anyone.

Leaning back on his chair he opened a cupboard below the bar counter and pulled out a leather pouch. He showed James his collection of twelve SIM cards before closing the cupboard and tossing the cards over to his friend.

"In my profession I often need to change numbers and operators." Johny said with a slimy smile.

"I thought you did real estate. That does need some consistent contact details. I am sure; your real estate shit is just a facade for some crook work you are doing," the cop in James was tipped off.

Johny laughed aloud. "I did real estate for a long time, but that and crook work is not mutually exclusive. A successful realtor is, more often than not, also a crook. I lost the taste for it when the markets got flatter and the guys I used to employ as hit men got together with the politicians I had bribed to start their own real estate companies. I have more interesting things to do now."

"Like?"

"Like what? I am a liaison manager for high profile individuals. I introduce people who do not know each other but might want to—for a handsome fee, of course! My clientele include some of the best known names in the country in all walks of life."

"What kind of needs?"

"We all have our needs. I surely have mine and, at some time during my real estate days, I found that I was spending a fortune on some of my requirements. Being my usual sharp self, I realised the opportunity for smart businessmen in this profession, so I plunged in. High risk appetite and extreme confidentiality with a penchant for innovation—that's me." Johny sat upright pulling up his imaginary collar.

"So you are pimping."

"No. That is crass. I am in a strategic business line. I have employees in five countries spanning four continents and clients all over the world. I run forty different websites and maintain four hundred odd profiles in social media, all with girls' names. At any given time there are fifty people on open chat forums from my virtual back office quietly selling our services. When it comes to personally contacting high profile clients, I deal with it." Johny took a sip from his glass and continued. "This is the oldest profession in the world where service was given in exchange for money or kind. This is a deterrent to rape and molestation of women. We only work with mutually consenting adults."

"You always had a passion for the illegal. You are lucky I am not in the department any longer."

"When I say high profile clients, your department is not an exception. Let me tell you something I have learned over time in my business: the uniformed guys are hornier than all others. They think fornication is their birth-right," He said like a sage. "The trouble is that they don't want to pay up."

James emptied his glass and snubbed his cigarette when Johny pulled a chair close to him and assumed a serious expression.

"I think I know someone who might be of help to you in this, near Nilambur."

"Who is it?"

"Abdul Rahman, a wily old bastard. He has contacts with some of the tribal folks and I am sure he would have got some scent of what is going on. By nature he is curious about anything suspicious as he himself survives on such nefarious activities."

"Do you think he will help, if he himself is a crook?" asked James

"He will if I ask him to. He canvases raw materials for me. You know there are connoisseurs of untouched stuff irrespective of the finish. People who only want virgins and are willing to pay anything to be the first one. Rahman gets me fresh tribal girls from Nilambur for my special clients."

"Pigs!" James shook his head but Johny laughed it off.

"We call him the Nilambur *Sultan*. The guy moves around like a fox, deals in hawala money, *ganja* and anything crooked that you can imagine. I will connect you to this devil only if you assure me that you will keep his secrets to yourself."

"Do I have an option?" said James

Johny took James' mobile and typed in Rahman's contacts and address.

"I will inform the guy today. Don't tell him about your police background at any point. You are a farmer friend of mine," Johny reminded.

James stood up and Johny walked him to the door.

"If you need anything, call. I can arrange for people, weapons, money or anything that you may need."

As they shook hands, Johny said gravely, "Jamie, do not trust anyone blindly in this operation. I have a feeling there is more to this iceberg than just the tip."

James looked him in the eye and saw the genuine concern of a friend. Smiling, he walked briskly to the lift lobby.

Once at the Kamaraj Domestic Terminal he called up Archbishop Matthias.

"Jamie, where the hell have you been? The buggers give us just twenty four hours. We have managed to get forty eight hours' time telling them there are certain formalities. The police, in principle, has accepted their demand but asked for more time so that they can plan their own counter attack

"I am in Chennai. We are moving tomorrow. Keep them engaged, let them know that we are willing to abide by their demands. I checked some of the online papers and it's all over the press," said James.

"I am sure the police will get at the criminals somehow but my fear is that they cannot secure the lives of the captives. I wonder if they are still alive," wondered the Archbishop.

"The police need to be prepared for the safe return of the hostages. It is very much possible that the gang is hiding in the forests. If so, the police have to be very careful. There would be landmines or suicide attacks and whatever else you can imagine," said James

"Yes. I am a worried man, James. Please call me when you have updates," said the Archbishop. "Bye for now."

"Bye."

12

Nilambur Sultan

James had to drive more than twenty kilometres through the hilly terrain, past large rubber estates, coffee and teakwood plantations to reach the small tile-roofed house of Nilambur Sultan. The roads were not paved well and half the distance there was no tarring, full of potholes and rocks. Rahman-the-fox lived on the bank of a giggling river with plenty of crystal clear water, healthy fish and water snakes. He fished when he had nothing fishy to do, which was rare.

Rahman was like the sap of rubber that dripped from the bark. Like the immaculately white but extremely sticky liquid, this man's simple and practically unnoticeable existence did not betray his illegal engagements.

He was a bachelor, unlike most Muslims who lived in the region. He was unsure of whether he had fathered any children but kept clear of marriages and divorces. He thought of such things as distractions for any creative, self-driven man. Unlike other Muslims who generally abstained from alcohol and pork, he enjoyed barbeque parties with pork meat and self-brewed arrack—often himself being the guest and the host. Occasionally he also entertained clients, skipping middlemen like Johny. This was rare, as he preferred to maintain a low profile, and went almost unnoticed by his neighbours and law enforcers. The few uniformed men who knew more than necessary were either on his payroll or had been his clients.

Now, in his early sixties, sitting in an easy chair on the veranda, he smiled at his visitor and gestured him to sit on the wooden stool right across from him.

"I don't like meeting people," he said calmly running his fingers through the thick hairs on his bare chest.

The Sultan wore a blue check dhoti with a thick belt holding it onto his belly. The dhoti was pulled up enough to reveal his long wiry legs.

"A friend of Johny is most welcome. He is one of the most professional guys I have dealt with, a man of his word—to the dot. It's hard to find such talents in my field," The Sultan leaned forward. "Can I make some black tea for you? And what's your name?"

"James. And don't bother with tea. I noticed you are here alone," said James.

"That's no big deal. We can talk in the kitchen, or do you prefer a fresh sip of home brewed arrack? It's made with gooseberries from our own forest," he spoke as if Nilambur forests were inherited by him.

"I will join you in the kitchen," James followed the half-naked Sultan into house. The man quickly washed a small aluminium pot, poured some water and placed it on the fire.

"What are you after?" Rahman took a *beedi* from the bunch tucked in his belt, lighted it in the stove and sucked hard to ensure that the fire would catch up. "Kaja *Beedi*," he offered blowing thick circles of smoke. James politely declined.

"A friend of mine was kidnapped along with some foreigners by naxals. They want to trade them for some notorious criminals in jail. This friend of mine and Johny's is who we are after," James gave him an account of what unfolded the day before and how he was keen to negotiate the release of his friend and the others that had been kidnapped.

The old man had heard of it from the television and newspapers.

"What makes you think that I can help?" He asked.

"Johny thought so. Actually he recommended strongly that I talk to you. He said you, in the confidential nature of your job, would have encountered information that could help me."

Rahman picked up a tin from the shelf and shook out a handful of tea leaves into his right palm, dropped the content into the wildly boiling water and dusted his palms together. Lowering the flame, he looked at James sharply.

"And *why* do you think I will help?"

"I don't know. I need to help a friend," James said, and added as an afterthought, "and because, I am Johny's friend."

The tea was poured into two glass tumblers and the aroma was tempting. They moved back to the veranda holding the hot tea glasses.

"I am willing to offer any reasonable remuneration for the help provided," James offered as he sat down and took a short sip which almost burnt his tongue. "The tea is good."

"I am not looking for any remuneration, what I want, I will ask in due time and you can offer me on friendship as I do for you now. What do you say?" Rahman smiled.

James nodded, even though he was not sure of when this guy might come up to him as ask him to do god-knows-what. Now he needed this fox and he may as well agree with him. "I suppose so. There is a time for everything."

Rahman sucked at the brink of the glass like a vacuum cleaner, closing his eyes tight, he enjoyed the hot tea in his mouth, the movements of his protruding Adam's apple indicating the transportation of the liquid down his throat. Pleased, he smiled showing off his uneven tobacco stained teeth. He took a last drag at the Kaja *beedi* and tossed the stub away into the court yard.

"I have been in touch with some tribal women from the forest, some of whom I have introduced to great careers in fabulous cities. They are physically very strong," he leaned back on his chair.

"There was a time when it was pretty common for landlords in the vicinity to hire them for weeks during high seasons and they took care of the farm and the farmer's needs. This generation is more ambitious and wants steadier employment and bigger income. Though their skin is darker than brown and their lips and noses are round and unattractive, they have the shapeliest bodies. They are ampler and firmer than any of the city girls you can get your hands on," The Sultan's palms cupped the imaginary figure in the air in front of him and James saw his eyes glitter.

Old bastard—James said to himself.

"I know that some of the men got involved in the movement, driven by the years of exploitation and by the hope of the kingdom of the poor that the naxalite leaders idealize. They had once thought that the Communist party would champion their cause but the party itself turned into the bourgeoisie. As you must have heard, *all are equal but some are more equal.* Under communist regimes in Kerala, the government workers enjoyed more and more benefits—with no accountability—the party leaders amassed personal wealth," he continued.

"I agree," said James.

"The naxalite movement has built training camps in our forest where they teach the use of various weapons as well as their revolutionary philosophy. The women are really scared of what will become of their men. They have grown up always in owe and fear of the landlords and the politicians. Some girls have told me that it is only a matter of time before the police kill their men, though I am not sure these girls are going to miss them much. They fend for themselves already and there are many men outside the forest who are willing to pay them for the little pleasures of life," Rahman took another vacuum cleaner suck from the tea glass and leaned back on the easy chair.

"Do you know where this camp is?"

"It's never at the same place for long. They move around in an area of six to ten kilometres on the eastern side of a hill about eight kilometres from here. There are no roads, only tribal pathways that are infested by wild animals, snakes and leeches. These folks are very good at moving around discretely, merging themselves to the surrounding foliage."

"Who trains them and how do *they* get to the camp site?"

"I don't know who they are. They come to the camp via various routes, never the same track twice. They would come via Ooty, Goodallur, Bandipur or any passage from the Kerala side."

"Have you seen them, the trainers?"

Sultan thought for a while pulling out another *beedi* and placing it between his teeth. James leaned forward and lit it with his lighter.

James took out a Kings from his pocket and lighted for himself.

"I suppose I have—a couple of times. They are in all shades and sizes, with some looking more urban than others but there's nothing extraordinary about them. I have a nose for anything strange and suspicious and I found out that they did meet some of the tribal men, who took them deep into the forests."

"Don't you think they should have more permanent havens if they stock weapons and ammunitions?" James asked.

"Yes. I don't know where it is but they would have safe places to hide them, use them for training and for real when the need comes. They also train on the use of poisoned arrows. I would not engage them if I were you. And they would protect their teachers like gods."

"I don't intend to fight them. I need to talk to them and reason with them."

"Best of luck!" Sultan laughed.

"Is there anyone that we can take with us who can help us contact the leaders?"

"No. I don't think I know anyone who would volunteer. The *adivasi* fighters are instructed by their naxalite leaders that any stranger is an enemy."

"Can we not entice, coerce or reason with them?"

Rahman dismissed it with a loud laughter. When he became serious again, he leaned forward and whispered, "I know one girl who might be able to help."

"A girl?" James was sceptical.

"Yes, a smart one. She has been curious about the camp and all that secrecy surrounding it. Once she trailed some men as they were leaving and managed to reach near the camp-site unnoticed. You bet she is one hell of a spy. She gave me good account of what happens there."

"Why do you think she will help us?"

"She won't help you or me for our sake but she has a score to settle and will do anything to get even."

"So there is a story to this woman?" James was now curious.

"Girl," corrected the Sultan. "According to her grandmother she was born a year after a major landslide in the Ghats which was about 18 years ago."

"Her uncle and brother are active in the naxalite camp and one of the teachers from the city visited her hut a couple times to meet her brother. One day this teacher managed to send the men off to some errant so that he was alone in the house with this girl."

"As soon as the men left the place, this man pounced on the poor girl like a hungry lion. Our girl was initially taken by surprise which worked as advantage to the bastard. Pulling her down on the floor, he was quickly over her pulling out her breast cloth. She pushed the guy away, picked up the harvesting sickle and charged at him. The wily asshole ran for his life and never returned. Unfortunately, her brother and uncle too did not return after that day. She thinks they have been murdered," stopped Rahman.

"I need to meet her. What is her name?" asked James.

"I think she is called Velli or something. You can name her anything when you meet her," Sultan got up from his easy chair and stretched himself.

"Can we meet her here tonight at ten or eleven? If you have time to brief her, please make sure she comes prepared for a few days of travel. That is, if she is willing to help," James said trying hard not to sound as giving instructions.

"OK. I will see you here tonight. Try not drawing attention of the local folks on your way. They have men all over the place," cautioned the old man.

"Noted."

13

Thou shall not fear

Nilambur Sultan had several rounds of home brewed arrack and was smoking a kaja *beedi* singing *"engane nee marakkum kuyile, engane nee marakkum"* in a reverie when a mini truck pulled up and four dhoti clad men descended near his house. The truck had some jute sacks of hay and dry cow dung and the loaders began to unload it all in his backyard.

Sultan was about to take out his Malappuram knife from the sheath tucked under the roof when he noticed the face of one of the loaders approaching him. It was James.

"What the hell is going on?" asked the agitated Sultan.

"Just some stuff for our long journey through the forest. These are my friends," said James.

"Are you guys going to be eating hay and cow dung? What strange tastes!" Sultan looked at James from top to bottom admiring the drastic transformation from the smartly dressed man who drank black tea with him that morning.

He was surprised to see the modern weapons being pulled out of the sacks and that under the soiled shirts the men wore bullet proof vests and pistol holders. There were nuts, dry fruits and meat, water bottles, chocolate bars, whole leaf tobacco, whisky and many such assortments in the bags.

A dark and short girl in tribal wear came out from one of the rooms in the house. She was stronger than James had imagined, and beautiful if not for the thick lips which were red from chewing betel leaves. When she smiled there was something attractive about her. The guys noticed that she wore no bra but resisted from staring at her firm pairs covered only by a thin breast cloth.

"No wonder the teacher went mad," whispered Joe in Avira's ear. James had already briefed them all about the girl.

Though she was sort of shy and silent at first when James and Rahman took her aside to make the introductions, Velli soon started talking and felt comfortable with James. Initially, it was hard for James to follow her *Paniya* dialect which he understood as a ping-pong version of Malayalam spoken in fast forward mode. She could understand the Travancore dialect that James spoke as she was familiar with the rich *nasrani* landlords in the area.

The whole team had a light dinner prepared by the Sultan himself. They washed it down with a dash of his home made arrack and slept for two hours before setting off on foot into the forest, towards Vavumala, just after one O'clock.

The pathway was comfortable for the first two kilometres but became steeper as it led to the deep woods. Velli moved fast and the four men had some trouble matching her sprightliness and speed as the terrain became tougher.

They avoided the path used by the tribesmen but moved parallel to it, keeping a safe distance.

Velli was the first to notice a herd of elephants moving majestically in the dark. Joe had imagined it to be some rocks. They lay silent till the whole herd went ahead of them and quietly advanced.

At various junctures, she would stop and motion them to stay still for a while, before moving along silently. They had covered several kilometres by five in the morning; then they sat down to drink some cold coffee. Vallie refused to have their coffee but drank some water from her dried Calabash shell. Through most of the trip she was silent, except occasionally when she informed James about the geography.

Joe was tempted to keep staring at her curves but concentrated on the uneven pathways and their cuts and curves instead. "Much better than the city girls", he mumbled under his breath and Avira elbowed him. "How long before we reach the camp?" Avira turned to Velli who had looked at the two mumbling men.

"Around five more hours to the place I saw last month, but they should have shifted," Said Velli. "There are two similar spots suitable for their type of camp an hour to the East and another to the North, down the hill."

"Do you mean towards Anackampoil?"

"I don't know what you call the place but it is near Vellarimala,"

The five member team continued their journey, sometimes sliding down the slopes or climbing up the rocks on all fours. They rubbed wet tobacco leaves on their calves and feet to ward off the leeches, which were ready to leap from the shoots of grass and dead leaves.

Leo carried the heaviest of the backpacks and had the maximum falls though others too slipped and fell; getting cuts and bruises all over. They were no strangers to blood; pain and difficulties only enlivened their enthusiasm on this expedition. After many years they were back on a dangerous mission!

Joe helped himself occasionally from the whisky bottle and imagined Velli in the costume of a fairy, then an angel and finally settled for a ramp-walking model in minimal costume. Then shrugging off the images he followed the others, swearing not to get drunk.

At around ten they ate chocolate and almonds and drank more coffee. James checked his cell phone and found there was still some signal in one of them, thanks to his ingeniously fitted signal booster.

He dialled Matthias. "Any news?"

"The police have almost completed the necessary formalities for the release of the prisoners. The guys have demanded that the prisoners be taken to a place on the Nilambur—Kakkadampoil road from where someone will join the team and direct them to the meeting place in the forest."

"I am sure they will meet far away from their camps but not too far so that they can have their resources mobilised in case of a full blown attack by the police. Were the National Security Guards called in too?"

"I do not know. The police are being very secretive about the whole thing. They have a commando force called Thunder Bolts specialised in jungle operations," said Matthias.

"We are already on the hunt and deep inside the forest. I probably won't have a signal from now on and it may not be secure enough to call you again. Pray for us!" said James.

"God be with you," James felt the assurance of his friend and hung up.

As they continued for another kilometre or so, James had the strange feeling that they were being observed. The team had been moving forward scanning three hundred and sixty degrees and making sure that there were no other humans around. Now his sixth sense made his neck tense and his eyes were darting all around.

Avira was taking a leak below a huge teak when he felt something grazing his neck. An arrow lodged itself on the tree inches away from him and all five fell to the ground, rolling until they found an obstacle to hide behind. Avira had no time to zip up and felt some sharp plant pocking him as he crawled behind the teak, his urine mixing with soil on his pants. The four men took a quick scan of ninety degrees in their respective directions and James heard a mild sound, like the opening of a soda bottle, followed by a scream and a thud. Leo's gun had fired and a diminutive man fell from a nearby tree breaking his neck on the fall. There was a long silence before Leo fired again and this time the scream came from behind a nearby bush. This was followed by the sound of someone running and in a sudden leap James fired, hitting the man on this calf.

When the team recouped they disarmed the wounded man and examined the other two.

"I didn't want bloodshed," Grunted James.

While they talked the tribal captive took a sudden lick at one of the arrows that lay near. Wish a sudden convulsion he fell flat on the ground, his eyes still open and staring at his attackers.

"Poisoned arrows, as expected," Avira rubbed his neck and thanked God. He had now zipped up and wished Velli had not noticed anything in the mayhem.

"We seem to be near the camp considering the presence of such an observation post—maybe another kilometre or two," Joe lighted a cigarette, took a deep drag and passed it to Avira.

"They would be on special alert considering the high profile kidnapping. We have to be stealthier," James took the cigarette from Avira.

"This is interesting!" James bent down by the corpse and pointed at the silver crucifix hanging from a black thread.

Velli pulled out a similar one from her own neck, which had not been noticed by the men before, as it safely rested in her cleavage and was covered by her clothes.

"Are you Christians? I thought Paniyas believed in Kali and Mariyamma.

"No, we were baptised by a visiting priest some years ago. They told us about Jesus and Mary and taught us prayers. We still continue our Paniyan rituals and practices but we get money and food from the Christians. But the *nasranis* still do not treat us as Christians, calling us *puthu*-Christians. Most of the teachers who train the tribal men are Christians too," said Velli.

"This is the case in many tribal areas in Jharkhand, Orissa, AP and Bihar. There has been several backlashes coming from the Hindu organisations against conversions. There are cases of persecution of the newly converts by some fundamentalist Hindus. Re-conversion drives, burning of missionaries and poisoning the wells of Christian dominated areas in Orissa are not uncommon. The missionaries that work with these *adivasis* have also drawn the ire of high castes and politicians," Leo contributed. One of his friends was involved in the investigation of the gruesome burning of a missionary family in Orissa.

James questioned her further about the priests who came to celebrate the holy mass for the tribal folks, to know if he could identify anyone. Her descriptions ended up being more about the colour of their skin and what they wore, than anything useful to him. He started regretting the fact that he hardly went to Church anymore and hadn't kept in touch with the clergy in his five years of exile in the farm.

After another hour of trekking—while James was surveying the area with his binoculars—he noticed a group of *adivasis* sitting along with a jeans-clad man below a huge rock. The city man had some papers rolled up which he held in his left hand and in his right one he had something like a chapatti roll. He was talking and the tribal folks were listening with apt attention.

"Have you seen this man before?" James whispered to Velli.

"No." she shook her head.

The attendees of the secret gathering were startled when they found guns pointing straight at their heads and four tough looking men ordered them to raise their hands in surrender.

Joe was quick to move closer and search them down and took away the pistol the city guy had tucked behind his back and couple of knives from the *adivasis*. He then proceeded to tie their hands and legs.

The Jeans-clad man had now recovered from the initial shock and knew he was under custody though not sure who his captors were.

"Who are you and why do you attack us like dacoits?" he asked the team. James had asked Velli to stay hiding behind the rocks, from where she kept observing them in absolute silence.

"We are friends of the guys you've kidnapped and we're here to take them back," said James.

"Who kidnapped who?" the man asked.

Avira was the one to answer this question. Moving closer the hefty ex-policeman jabbed the guy with butt of his rifle in the abdomen. Groaning, the man fell to his knees.

"We don't want anybody to get hurt but if you guys do anything stupid, we know how to deal with you. So let us talk business. Let us ask the questions now and you jolly well will answer them," Avira raised the man's chin with the barrel of the gun.

"I am a teacher of the *adivasis*. I only know that some big guys have been kidnapped and we are trying to get some of our colleagues released from jail but I don't know anything else," he pleaded.

"If you love your life, there are two questions we need answers for. If not, neither we nor this world has any use for you," threatened Avira.

The teacher broke into a mocking laughter. "Do you think I am afraid of dying? When we got into this we all knew that someday we'd have to face the bullets. The cause is noble enough to give up my life. That won't stop the voice of the hundreds of the downtrodden," He stood up composed.

"And don't take me for a fool. I know you are the Police. The weapons and your style of operation make that pretty clear. I do not know who you work for—Kerala Police or SPG or even the Army. Friends of some priests walking around with sophisticated handguns! You can't fool even the *adivasis* with this story."

James, who was so far quiet, moved forward and touched the man on the shoulder so he would look him in the eye.

"We are not from the police or have any official sanction. We are as illegal as I think you are. We are, in fact, supporters of the movement for the liberation of the poor and want the saying "blessed are the poor" to become a reality," James paused.

"We get these weapons from similar sources as you do, through parallel trade arrangements. Frankly, we are not concerned about all of the priests that have been kidnapped. It's just that one of them, the Indian priest, Zacharia Tharakan, is a special friend of mine and I want him back unhurt."

James noticed that the mention of Zach's name wiped off some animosity from the eyes of the man and that encouraged him. "I only need to know who I should talk to about securing his release. I know the police are negotiating the release of the Italians but in case of any foolishness from their part, I do not want anything to happen to my friend."

"Will you help us talk to anyone who can negotiate the release of Fr. Zacharia?" James asked.

"Yes, but you'll have to trust me. Can I make a call?" asked the teacher who had now become more amiable.

"How will you do that? There seems to be no network here," said Joe.

"There are wireless networks and I have some equipment hidden nearby. If you let me, I can get in touch with my leaders. Maybe they will let you talk to your friend," offered the man.

James looked at his friends whose expressions indicated that they trusted him to make the best decision.

"I guess I'll have to trust you," he said.

The teacher pointed at a large stone and hidden under the dry leaves Joe found the wireless unit. He picked it up and examined it to make sure it wasn't an explosive or a detonator, before handing it back to James.

James untied the teacher's hands and gave him the device.

"Shaun on line, can you hear?" After a while a reply came.

"Yes, what's the matter?" said a voice in chaste Tamil.

"I have a situation. Don't say anything until I finish speaking. I need to talk to the elder," he said hurriedly in Tamil.

"Yes. I'll get him on line," said the voice on the other end and James understood that the man in front of him must not be such a small link in the chain, if he can get access to the senior leaders this easily.

"It's me. What's the problem?" asked a powerful voice on the other end.

"We got into the hands of four infiltrators and are now in their custody. Don't disconnect, let me finish."

"Police?"

"No. They claim to be friends of Fr. Zacharia Tharakan and want to negotiate his release unofficially."

"Why should we talk to them? Are they threatening to kill you?"

"I don't care about dying but I feel they are genuine and want to talk. But they are armed."

"Why should we talk to them? We are already negotiating with the police."

James heard some whispers at the other end before the speaker again came on line. "Who do they say they are? Any identification?"

The teacher now looked at James and responded "Let me check".

"Tell them my name's James. Here is my driving licence. I am a farmer," James showed him his licence.

"James is the name. Showed me his driving licence, it's not fake," The teacher spoke.

There was a prolonged silence at the other end before the wireless came live again.

"Bring them here but without all their arms and ammunitions. Get them here clean if they want to talk."

"Will they not take us hostages as well, if we go there without our guns?" asked Leo.

"You have to trust us. If you are what you say you are, you have nothing to fear," said the teacher.

"I think we have no option. But we refuse to let you carry any of these as well. And you can't tell anyone where we have left the weapons. We need to take them back with us when we return. A gentleman's deal," said James.

The teacher thought for a while before calling his leader about James' proposal. Surprisingly, the other agreed. "Bring them with due respect, do not harm them," was the order.

Placing the wireless in his pocket and collecting his scattered papers, the teacher looked at the four men.

One by one they put down all their weapons and ammunitions under the huge rock and covered them with twigs and leaves. The teacher then checked each of them from head to toe and when he was satisfied he started walking. "Follow me."

14

Liberation camp

The four men continued their journey with the full knowledge that, if their trust was betrayed, these could very well be their last few hours of existence. But then again, they were in it together and that gave them courage.

After another two hours of gruelling trekking they saw the camp-site at a distance. As they approached the epicentre they noticed several *adivasis* perched on the top of the surrounding trees, camouflaged by the thickness of leaves.

Some men walked up to receive them and addressed the teacher as 'sir', which was a sign of respect and revealed his high position in the hierarchy. 'All are equal but some are more equal,' thought James.

They were taken near one of the many small tent-like structures, mostly made of tarpaulin and bamboos. Though most men there were armed with rifles, machine guns and bows and arrows, the tent housed no weapons.

There was a water pot and a coconut shell that could be used as cup.

"Welcome, James Mathew IPS and your famous band of deputies," said the powerful voice of the well-built man who walked in to the tent. It was James' and his friends' turn to be startled. They had never seen the man before.

"Who are you? How do you know us?" asked James.

"Who doesn't know you? You became a household name among the entire movement when you captured some of our best men and killed many of our cadres," continued the man.

"I am the new southern commander. They call me the elder. Five years ago I was still an activist and there was hardly any reason why you should know me. Back then I ran the north Kerala unit," he had a shining Glock 17 tucked to his belt but did not appear to have any interest in using it now.

"You don't know how I supported your cause after the capture then. These men and I walked out of the service in protest because the government refused to implement the developmental programmes for the poor villagers of Sathyamangalam. You have misunderstood us!" James said, really meaning his words.

The elder smiled.

"If we had misunderstood, you and your friends would not be alive right now. We would have hunted you down wherever you were and found a way to eliminate you. Even now, the first thing I would have done at the sight of you would have been to empty this into your heads," he pointed at the Glock.

"On the contrary, we know you had sympathies for our cause and that you really thought you were doing what was best for the people we are fighting for. You wanted to fight the system while being part of it but failed miserably," He said.

James was again surprised by how well informed the guy was and thought he was really capable of planning his and his team's elimination if he really wanted to. It was easy to have planted a bomb in the farm house or individually bumped them off when they went about their carefree life.

"Since you know all of this, will you let me talk to my friend? Is he safe?" asked James.

He motioned to the teacher with a tilt of his head as he led James and team outside the tent.

There were four tents of different sizes and, with a quick scan of the area, James saw approximately twenty-five men in the camp. He estimated that four times that number would have been stationed in the paths leading to the camp and around the area where they intend to meet the police to exchange the prisoners.

Most of the men were assembled in a semicircle with a radius of ten metres around where the team now stood with the elder.

James was not too far away from a tent guarded by four armed militants.

The teacher first emerged, and standing aside, held the curtain open. In the fading lights James could not see what was inside the tent but soon recognised the fair skinned priest who walked out dressed in a handloom *kurta* and blue jeans.

There was no sign of bruises or struggle on his body and his face was as handsome as ever.

"My friend!" exclaimed Zacharia as he walked forward to greet James with open arms.

James was so relieved that his friend looked healthy despite his many days in captivity. The captors seem to have treated him kindly, his clothes were fresh and he showed no sign of fatigue.

The two remained in embrace for a minute, during which James realised that he still liked Zach. Around ten years had gone by since they had last hugged, when James left the seminary. His heart had beaten as fast as it did now. He had missed his friend for several weeks after that but the rigour of preparing for the civil services examinations and subsequent training days had helped James overcome the pain of separation.

Now the two friends stood looking at each other genuinely happy to meet again. Zach held James' hand tightly, "I knew you would come for me."

James felt a lump in his throat and fought back an urge to hug his friend again.

Then, in a moment, he was again the cop who had to calculate his next move. He noticed that may be owing to his priesthood for many years, Zach displayed a level of calmness that did not betray the condition he was in. Many years ago, in much less threatening circumstances, he would have freaked out.

It is easier to rescue a calm and composed man than one who panics, James' police instincts assured him.

He was surprised that the elder and other armed men kept a distance and did not interfere with the emotional reunion. Joe, Leo and Avira stood nearby, looking at one another. They had already scanned their surroundings with their hound-like eyes, smelling for every danger that lay around.

"There are so many things I need to ask you, but I'm not sure where to begin," James looked at the smiling priest again.

"I have many things to tell you as well. This meeting was in God's plans," replied his friend.

"Are you as well as you appear to be? What have they done to you? Where are the other prisoners?"

"I am as well as I could be. These men have been taking good care of me. The other two are safe, but locked up in one of the tents."

James now turned to the elder, "what do I have to do for you so that I can take my friend away safely?"

"Release our leaders," said the Elder with an ironic smile.

"I will negotiate with the police and get them to you. I am in touch with some of the highest authorities. Let me take Father Zacharia with me for now and you can keep the other prisoners with you until I bring your leaders here," said James.

"Smart! Really smart!" laughed the elder. "You leave now; gather more forces and arms to stealthily attack the camp after your friend has been rescued. That is not going to happen."

"Can we have some seats for our guests, please?" said Zach looking at the teacher and James was surprised at the ease with which he went about in his captivity. In no time six bamboo stools were brought in. The elder and Zach took their seats and motioned the four visitors to sit as well.

"James, my friend," said Zach, "what everyone here wants of you is very straightforward."

"What is that?"

"That you join the movement," said Zach

"What?" James did not understand.

"The movement needs a leader as vibrant and capable as you to lead *us* to the final revolution that we've been preparing for decades." said Zach.

"Why do your advocate their demand, Zach? Is this Stockholm syndrome or something like that?" James asked.

"Because the present Head of the Naxalite movement in India wants you to take on the executive leadership of the movement," said the elder.

"Who is he?"

"I am!" said Father Zacharia Tharakan looking his friend straight in the eyes.

For a moment James could not believe what he heard, nor could any of the other three men. This was not a scenario they could have even hypothesised.

Then everything began to fall into place, the kidnapping, the safe custody and his friend's behaviour.

"James, you are one of the best I have seen in strategy, execution and temperament. There is no other. If you join us, along with the five men we are going to get released, we can work miracles in this country. We can put an end to the centuries of subjugation of many tribal folks and poor in our country. I can provide them moral leadership and Christian courage but you know I am neither a fighter, nor a born leader as you are! You know I have always looked up to you." Zacharia was now animated.

"You are a priest of the Catholic Church. How could you be the leader of an armed militant revolution?"

"Militancy is only a means to a desirable end. You pray that 'Your kingdom come'. What is His kingdom? Is it the one ruled by corrupt and greedy men, where rich become richer and all the poor are doomed? Jesus was a revolutionary. He was the first communist the world ever saw. The early Christians practiced it—each according to his ability and need. Is the hoarding up of wealth by a few and the exploitation of all the rest the kingdom of God that Jesus envisioned? No, James. If we do not throw out this system and establish an administration that follows the noble teachings of the Lord, we are not men of God!" Zach had gotten up and was gesturing passionately.

"Is this not a Christianised version of Marxism? Communism has failed in most parts of the world. The ones that still survive are the skeletons of Marx with flesh of the Bourgeoisie," James argued. "And how can the official Church accept this?"

"It is not the institution of the Catholic Church that has created this movement in any part of the world. The revolutionary praxis of the people of God has always been built through bottom-up movements. Yes, Church does support the conversion of these poor *adivasis*. If they continue being exploited, what is the point in them converting? Don't you remember when we were unceremoniously bundled off from Andhra Pradesh by the official Church for trying to help the downtrodden?" Zach stood akimbo.

"The official Church, both by commission and omission, supports the existing institutions and presides over the exploitation of the poor. In trying to protect the ecclesiastical and political order, the Church neglects the basic teachings of the Lord," said Zacharia.

"I agree that the Church has joined forces with the rich. But, be practical Zach. This will never succeed. The political and administrative structure of India will not allow any armed revolutionary movement to gain momentum. It will be crushed easily and emphatically by the state forces," James tried to convince his friend.

"Are you afraid to lead this charge? There are countries like China and Venezuela that are willing to put their might behind this struggle. They will legitimise it when it is big enough. For that we need leaders like you to march in front of an army of God's people towards the strongholds of Indian democracy! There are people around the world willing to contribute with donations, arms and support at international forums. Isn't it practical enough?" Zach explained.

"I cannot accept or justify violent killings, kidnappings and attacks on innocent police personnel that the naxals have unscrupulously indulged themselves in over the years. If you lay down arms and fight your cause through democratic means, I'll be there to support you," James made his stand clear.

"James! Please try to understand. I have dedicated my life to this and I will not desert the movement until I see the day we succeed!" Zach was eloquent even in pleading.

"Zach! Please come with me," It was now James' turn to plead with his friend. "Let us forget this whole story; no one knows you were involved. Return to the real world."

"I am not going with you. If you will not join the movement, then you are against us! I am sorry for you," Zach threw his hands up.

The elder now got up and came nearer to the four gentlemen. "What becomes of you now?"

James continued to address Zach. "Please release the other two prisoners and let us go back now."

"Sorry, Mr. James," it was the elder who answered. "We are not releasing the two Italians, we need our leaders back here. Father Zacharia has made that crystal clear."

James observed that there were six men guarding the only tent that his team had not had a good view of. He imagined that the prisoners should be in there.

"Zach! I need to take these Italians back to Matthias." James shouted.

"Do you think we would let you do that? We are now seriously thinking of not letting you go back. You now know too much about us," said the elder. There were several clicks and James saw five men aiming their guns at them and waiting for the order.

"How can I kill you my friend? And how can I let you live now?" Father Zacharia walked up to James, who had gotten up. James knew his friend had become a fanatic and that his expressions bordered abnormality. There were tears in his eyes when he looked at James with compassion, but those eyes also betrayed the command they held for the gun-men.

"They die here and now!" The elder said.

"Let us give some more time for my friend James. Maybe he will change his mind when he sees the fate of his friends," said Zach. "Tie them up and shoot them!" He ordered, and turning around, hurried back into the tent accompanied by his bodyguards.

The elder now motioned for some of the men surrounding James and his friends to go tie their hands.

"This is not right! We came here because you promised us that we can negotiate," protested Joe.

"We will ensure that your leaders are set free in exchange of the two Italians," James offered.

"Your involvement will not make any difference, gentlemen. We are dealing with the police on this and we know what to do with the Italians once we get our leaders back," the Elder laughed aloud. The four men looked at each other.

James looked around and knew that they were now surrounded by people who loved to kill. It was written all over their face—there were rare maniacs in the world that would kill for the pleasure of killing. Causes were just excuses to justify the satisfaction of their primeval need to torture and murder.

He saw it in the eyes of the elder. The man was now smacking at the thought of finishing off the unarmed men that stood before him.

Then, as if drunk by the merriment of the expected execution, the man they called elder turned maniac, laughing again at the thought of bloodshed—in the past and in the future. People like him only could blast bombs on women and little children—in schools, buses and trains.

"We have seen blood, haven't we?" he asked in jest and his men laughed.

Then he turned to the ex-cops and brought his face close to theirs in a cruel smile. "You want the Italians? The assholes were becoming such a pain while moving from one camp to the next, howling and wailing all the while!"

"You killed them?" James shouted staring at him and the man recoiled.

"Long ago . . . ! Shot and buried somewhere deep in the woods. You and the Police are on a wild goose chase!" elder turned to the teacher. "What are you waiting for? Tie up these devils!"

He then suddenly fell silent as his eyes popped out and a croak sound came from his throat. The elder slumped to the knees before falling sideways to the ground, his eyes still fixed on James. An arrow had neatly entered from his back and cut straight through his now silent heart.

There was chaos as the gun-men tried to figure out what exactly had happened. Those few seconds were enough for James and his friends to drop down and roll away behind the stones and trees that could shield them from gun shots.

While some men converged to the elder's dead body, many began to spread out with their arms drawn. James was the first to see Velli behind a huge tree, as he had taken shelter behind a large stone nearby. It was almost dark and it was impossible for anyone else to spot her.

She motioned with her eyes to the large pile of weapons some twenty feet from where she stood. She had carried their weapons with her as she followed the four men and the naxalites to the camp—stealthily trailing them.

There was another cry when Velli fired a second arrow and another man fell, creating further commotion. James used this confusion to crawl quickly towards the weapons and pick up an automatic rifle and his pistol. He then moved clockwise and took position behind a rock, firing mercilessly at the men holding the guns.

Having identified a target, the men began to fire back in James' direction. Taking advantage of the distraction, the rest of his team managed to get a hold of their weapons.

Avira threw a grenade into the tent where he had seen a cache of ammo and a deafening blast followed. Limbs flew and fire leaped to the sky, burning leaves and branches along the way. Many left their bows and arrows and began running away, in an effort to save their lives, while others, deranged by the powerful blast ran amok screaming and laughing.

James was not sure whether his friends were still safe as some ten gunmen took positions on the other side of the camp and engaged them with equal fervour.

As tents caught fire, many men ran out into the woods in the opposite direction. The four men never fired at any one who was running away, targeting the armed men instead. Leo had succeeded in shooting down five of them and two others ran out of ammunition and fled. In the next half hour the entire resistance had died down.

There were four bodyguards with their guns pointing at all directions outside Zach's tent, while Zach himself never came out. The only other tent that had withstood the blast and gunshots was now set ablaze by another one of Avira's grenades. Joe and Leo had changed their positions several times, misleading the enemy. Avira then landed straight in front of the four men guarding the tent with his automatic spitting bullets. There was no time for them to open fire as they were being sprayed by bullets. The only shots fired by one of them, as he was falling, strayed into the woods.

James, Joe and Leo joined him in a formation that covered all directions as they entered the tent, aiming their guns straight at the only surviving body guard who stood near Zacharia.

"Drop your gun!" shouted Leo pointing his Glock straight at the man's forehead. "Duck!" Leo shouted when, instead of dropping the gun, the guard aimed it straight at them with menacing fury in his eyes. Leo's bullet had struck him on the forehead before he could dispatch a single bullet from his automatic.

The weapon and the man fell down in a heap near Zach's feet.

James could not imagine how his seminary friend stood so calm amidst that kind of violence. He could feel his own pulse rising, even though he was familiar with such encounters.

"Do not try any tricks, Father!" Joe warned, aiming at Zacharia. "James may have a soft corner for you but none of us share that feeling! We treat all criminals alike."

Zacharia only smiled mockingly.

"Tie him up," said James. Avira came forward and tied the hands of the passive priest, who kept his sarcastic smile amidst all the commotion.

The team slowly moved out, James leading Zach by his hand while the others scanned all directions with their guns cocked and ready to fire at any sign of hostility. As they moved away from the tent, Avira threw a burning log on the roof of the lone tent, which immediately caught fire. The sun had now set but the flames kept the woods alight and the men moved faster into the darkness.

They were joined by Velli, who had kept herself in hiding, ready to provide cover for the men in action.

"You are the fifth man in our team! You understood that the arms we laid away were meant to be collected and you kept trailing after us without us having to say anything at all," Joe whispered to her as they walked side by side. She smiled at him and passed on a ripe mango. He took it and started eating as the entourage scaled their way back.

She then fished in her shoulder sack and pulled out his whiskey bottle with a naughty smile. Joe took it from her and threw her a flying kiss. He thought he saw her blush in the darkness.

Zach just walked in silence. Maybe he knew he would be shot if he made any attempt to escape.

After walking for two kilometres or so, they found a huge rock standing like a gigantic elephant. They halted there for a while to drink water, clean their wounds and apply tobacco on their skins before moving forward.

Then, with a sudden impulse, Zacharia ran up the rock. Leo was quick to get his gun and take aim. "Stop or I fire!" He screamed.

James motioned to his men that they should hold their fire but Leo kept his gun aimed at Zach, who looked back but kept walking up. Then, with a loud cry, he jumped down to the steep side of the rock, hitting the ground twenty feet below with a loud blast. The rock split in parts, the earth flew up some fifteen feet, stones and soil thrown all around in the explosion.

"Landmine! He knew where it was," shouted Joe. They ran down only to find Zacharia's lifeless body scattered in all directions, along with splinters of rock and mud.

James sat down with his head sunk in his palms. He said nothing while looking at the ground near his feet, avoiding the sight of his dead friend. Zach had once been a petit, girlish looking, curious and loving boy whose friendship James had cherished. Now, a failed revolutionary and wavered priest, he lay still at his self-made altar for the liberation of God's people.

James' friends stood near him in silence for a while. Avira pressed his shoulder and when James looked up indifferently, he offered him a hand. James stood up holding it. The four men and the *adivasi* girl walked back in silence as the forest once again returned to its usual eeriness.

The long and miserable wailing of a fox could be heard at a distance. Chirping of crickets and loud crocking of frogs filled the night air. All around them, trees and shrubs—tall and short—stood dark and silent, like ghosts, waving their arms in the descending fog.

James crossed himself and said a silent prayer.

Epilogue

Archbishop Matthias woke up early. He had only slept for two-three hours. Getting into his cassock he switched on the Television. In the past three days, most of his time was spent in speaking—to his superiors in Rome, to the police and to the reporters who hung around the Archbishop's house—watching news channels on TV and reading newspapers.

The early morning news announced the dramatic end to the kidnapping of Vatican delegates.

"The high profile kidnapping of the Vatican diplomats and an Indian priest came to a tragic end with all three captives being killed. In a daring operation, following the information that the captives were dead, the Thunder Bolt team of the Kerala Police attacked and killed thirty hard-line naxalites and destroyed their camp-site.

The DGP was shown addressing the media, "Our team was on their way to the meeting place, where we had agreed to hand over the under trail activists, when through reliable intelligence we learned that the naxals had already killed the priests. We also learnt that they operated camps to train *adivasis* the use of fire arms. They were planning to attack several civilian targets."

"While we are deeply saddened by the death of three priests of the Catholic Church at the hands of the terrorists, their kidnapping and death has led to the revelation of sinister designs of the naxals," said Home Minister Vasudevan Menon in Thiruvananthapuram.

Then came up his own statement.

"I am saddened by the death of the three priests. I have lost a friend and batch mate in Father Zacharia Tharakan, a vocal advocate of the poor. He was instrumental in many initiatives to help the poor in our diocese. He practiced poverty in its extreme, often skipping food and spending days and nights among the poor in their own abject conditions," said the Archbishop.

Now the news continued, "Father Zacharia's funeral would be held with all honours in his native parish in Nilambur on Saturday presided over by the Archbishop."

Matthias closed his eyes "Mysterious are your ways, O Lord!"

Miles away in the farm James and his friends opened a bottle of rum.